ATLANTA'S GUIDE TO CRYPTIDS

BOOK ONE OF THE DRC FILES

KEVIN A DAVIS

Inkd Publishing

Copyright © 2023 by Kevin A Davis

All rights reserved.

No part of this book may be reproduced in any form or by any electronic or mechanical means, including information storage and retrieval systems, without written permission from the author, except for the use of brief quotations in a book review.

Cover art Mibl Art

For April
Always April. She gives me balance in my life which is sorely needed considering my usual hectic pace.

In Memory of David Farland.
A guiding teacher who was always passionate about mentorship and writing. You are loved and missed.

ATLANTA'S GUIDE TO CRYPTIDS

CONTENTS

Introduction	ix
Chapter 1	1
Chapter 2	5
Chapter 3	15
Chapter 4	26
Chapter 5	39
Chapter 6	52
Chapter 7	67
Chapter 8	82
Chapter 9	94
Chapter 10	107
Chapter 11	115
Chapter 12	123
Chapter 13	130
Chapter 14	139
Chapter 15	150
Chapter 16	160
Chapter 17	168
Chapter 18	178
Chapter 19	195
Also by Kevin A Davis	231
Acknowledgments	233

INTRODUCTION

This is the story of Kristen Winters, first a mother, also a witch, and formerly a lead detective for the police force in Grand Junction.

She thought she'd taken a new job with the FBI, right up until she met her new coworkers. New on the team, it's time for a crash course on exactly what kind of dangerous cryptids can end up crawling out of the realms.

Welcome to the Department of Realm Containment. Caution: small, short elements of horror may occur (there are cryptids after all), but it's actually a light-hearted paranormal procedural with even doses of action and mystery set in modern day Atlanta.

CHAPTER ONE

Heather Norris corralled three dawdling third graders from her class toward the Tutankhamen exhibit where her other students chattered. A typically sedate and quiet woman in her day-to-day life, she'd jogged around the museum enough that sweat dotted her forehead under brown hair, and her blue blouse stuck to her sides with a rising hint of funk.

Her voice, hoarse from too much use, grated with a version of her teacher's tone. "Stephanie, come back to the group. We'll all be going to see the Nile after we learn about King Tut." An earthy odor hung in the air, likely from the desert sand ahead.

Stephanie's dark, braided pigtails swung as she glanced back with a smile, pointing past the small Egyptian boat and fishermen. "A naked mummy."

Heather frowned as she found a gray man stepping from a hidden door at the far edge of the exhibit. That corner had little more than sand and plants, as if hinting at the edge of an oasis in the desert. From her vantage, fake palms hid all but his splotchy face and sunken eyes. Her pulse rose as she hesitantly stepped toward Stephanie. "It's just . . ." The museum must have had some interactive event planned.

His lips peeled up from his top teeth in an odd way. His arms and legs moved in halting, ungainly jerks so that his gait appeared disturbingly inhuman. Heather reached Stephanie and paused as she aimed a hand toward the nine-year-old's shoulder. The gray man stumbled another step, leaving the sand-colored door ajar and providing ample proof that he wore no clothes. "Sh—" Heather cut off her curse and dropped a tense hand onto Stephanie's shoulder. "C'mon." A quick search proved there wasn't one member of the museum's staff, or anyone other than her students, in the room.

The man moved erratically as Heather turned Stephanie toward the class. Dark blotches covered gray skin. His head swiveled unnaturally and locked on her. Shriveled gray lumps drew back into his skull, creating dark pits which replaced his eyes. Heather gasped; panic climbed into her chest. "Back to the . . ." She couldn't think where they'd just been. "Ice cream — in the lobby." She gestured toward the museum's wide arch of an exit from the Egyptology exhibit. "Hurry."

The gray man, a walking corpse, stumbled toward her. His legs spread, he didn't move quickly at first. His mouth opened wider causing the top lip, stuck to the bottom, to rip more and expose gray teeth and dark gums.

Heather shrieked. Stephanie stood at her side, entranced. The rest of the class had turned abnormally silent.

"Run," Heather whispered.

The corpse faltered on a low rise of sand, but it was picking up speed. It couldn't see, not without eyes. Still, its dark sockets focused on Heather. She had to get the children out. The odor of her own sweat rose over the stale dry air in the room.

"Run!" Heather screamed. She spun, pushing first Stephanie, then anyone she could reach. Her students were gawking, jaws open and even pointing. "Run!"

Stephanie backed up one step, her mouth opening as if to make a comment. Heather twirled the girl by her shoulders and pushed her into the others.

Dull feet slapped on tile behind her. Heather's throat choked, but she couldn't get the children to move. "Run," she pleaded with a croak.

One of her children screamed, then another. The corpse's fleshy footsteps smacked on the floor. With Heather's next breath, she inhaled the reek of rotting flesh wafting in the air. Even as the first child finally sped for the door, she knew she couldn't follow; too many hesitated.

"Run!" Skin cold and goosebumps rising on her neck, she turned to face the horror, spreading her arms protectively in front of the children behind her.

It was a corpse. An impossible, horrible, angry animation of flesh bore down on her. She couldn't help but draw in short breaths, inhaling its stench. The torn flesh around the mouth flapped loosely. Gray teeth hung from nearly black gums.

The children turned into a screaming chorus racing away from her. Someone fell and cried, but she dared not turn. Heather braced for the impact. She expected the corpse to topple into her. Instead, it lumbered to a quick stop and punched into her stomach.

Heather fell back a step, but not as far as she expected. The nightmare creature held her somehow.

The corpse's flesh rolled up like loose cuffs around its forearm. She blinked at the impossible image. A slight tug registered in her stomach, and dark blood seeped into the blue of her blouse. Her own foul smell of viscera joined the miasma. Again, she tried to step back, managed half a step, and finally felt the raging pain in her mid-section.

Her skin screamed and ripped as the corpse removed its hand. White ligaments and darker muscle clung to the bones of its wrist. Its skin had peeled back from the impact. White bones of the corpse's fist clutched her pink intestines.

Heather stumbled back, tethered by her yellow-tinged innards, and screamed.

CHAPTER
TWO

The lettering on the glass said "DRC." Google had taken me to the FBI building just fine, but navigating to the office had been a room-to-room search. I opened the door with a slow, careful push and peered inside.

"You must be the fresh blood, Kristen Winters." His voice rich and crooning, the pale man had a handsome smile and wore a dark, expensive suit which molded impeccably to his thin but solid frame.

The office was deep; filing cabinets lined the left side, and along the right, a row of three desks spaced widely apart faced me. A familiar, faint, putrid odor wafted amid the electrical scent of computers and printers. In the back, a door stood between two tinted windows. The only other occupant, a man with a welcoming grin and black dreads to his shoulders, rose from the back desk.

I tensed and forced a smile despite the fresh blood comment, which I assumed hinted at my new or probationary status. "Yes, Kristen Winters. I'm supposed to report to the ASAC Marie Pyre." The door at the back had lettering too small to read and blinds pulled down. I'd expected a larger team.

The pale man stepped forward and offered his hand. Dark brown hair draped halfway down his back; he'd tied it at the nape of his neck. "Special Agent David McCree." As he waited for me to shake his hand, his eyes smiled, as if he were telling me a joke.

As I touched his cold flesh, the black realm of Tarus glimmered at his shoulders. He'd known I was a witch. David would realize that my witch sensitivities would see the Tarus realm on touch and thus expose him as a vampire. He had wanted me to react, and I probably had. My already rattled nerves spiked.

"Cold hands," I said, not pulling away. At least I could identify the smell now.

He beamed as though I'd passed some test of his. His "fresh blood" comment left me some idea of his sense of humor. "The oafish witch behind me is our beloved SSA, Finn," David said.

Happily, I released David's hand and focused on the other agent whose long strides ate up the distance between us. Where I'd wrongly assumed David to be in his late thirties — a vampire could be centuries old — Finn looked to be in his forties. He wore a simple black jacket and pants like myself, though he wore no tie, and his white shirt opened at the neck to accentuate his rich brown skin. He stood perhaps a half a foot taller than my curvy five-foot-five-inch figure, so I had to tilt my head to meet his eyes.

"Finn Billings. I'm the other witch on the team. It'll be good to have someone to talk with." His eyes flicked toward the vampire with more humor than malice. Finn wore a pleasant, spicy aftershave.

"Kristen." I flushed lightly. They obviously knew my name.

CHAPTER TWO

I glanced at the three desks. Finn had risen from the farthest one in the back with pens and papers neatly organized. A framed picture, office phone, keyboard, mouse, and monitor each had their proper place.

The middle desk had a make-up mirror next to the screen and miscellaneous clutter strewn from one end to the other. The closest to the front looked empty save for the computer equipment. "The last agent wasn't a witch?" I asked.

"Merfolk." David rattled strong-scented mints in a red and white tin. "Nearly as bad." He offered me one as he raised a single eyebrow.

I shook my head to David's offer and didn't ask what had happened to the previous agent. There were plenty of merfolk here on Earth from their watery realm, but I'd only met two that I knew of. "I should check in." Nudging my chin toward the back door, I took a deep breath. "Is she in?"

David plucked out a mint. "Knock first." Dark gums accented his sharp cuspids as he tossed the white candy into his mouth. He smiled, lips closed, and looked exotically handsome again.

I'd been assigned to an unusual team with a vampire and a witch. The entire morning had been spent going through non-disclosures and other paperwork, which made a lot more sense now that I'd met some of the team. I strode toward the rear of the office, patting at random black curls that frizzed toward my cheeks. A whiteboard with grisly pictures had been tucked partially behind the end cabinet. Banker's boxes rested on the gray tops, and a pile grew from the floor. My heart still beat fast since finding a vampire on my new team. Heading for the door to meet my new boss didn't slow my pulse. I hadn't been looking to join the FBI, but I would have been crazy to pass up an opportunity like this. Clutching my purse strap with my left hand, I absently twisted my hair during the last two steps.

I straightened my back and rapped two confident knocks with my knuckle.

"Don't knock, dammit. Just come in." The woman's voice, Marie's I assumed, sounded mildly annoyed.

Sinking slightly, I refused to look back at David. I'd have to watch out for his pranks. I'd been the new officer a couple times.

I stepped inside and frowned at the scent of incense. Brightly lit, the office was almost as large as the other room. The outer office had been cool while here warmer air surrounded me, but we *were* in Atlanta. Wooden shelves covered every surface, even the tinted windows, and books and mementos filled every available space. A round polished table sat at the far end with four chairs. An ancient red and gold sofa pressed against shelves to my right. A massive dark stained desk dominated the middle of the room, and my new bald-headed boss sat behind the monitor there.

Marie rose, only slightly taller than me. "Welcome to Pyre's Pups." Her light brown scalp shone as she tilted her head, gesturing for me to sit on the couch. "You'll know when it's a bad time to come into the office. Knocking won't make it better." She had a pleasant face though I couldn't place her age. Her curves rivaled my own.

"Well, okay . . ." I swallowed. "Kristen Winters." My hand came off my purse strap on the way past her desk, but I resisted touching the ornate edges. "I was told to report to you."

She frowned when I sat in the middle of the sofa and waved me over so she could join me. Her dark brown eyes studied me until I averted mine. "What have they told you about our team?" Marie asked.

I curbed my initial reaction and didn't complain about the odd secrecy that had surrounded my recruitment. "Very little. An FBI team that deals with dangerous elements." When they'd recruited me, I'd just returned from medical leave after my encounter with a drug-addled werewolf. I had assumed a connection.

Marie shifted one knee onto the couch to face me and steepled her fingers in her lap. "We're not FBI." She rolled her eyes at the room. "Convenient cover for our little group. We deal with a higher authority than the US government."

I didn't blurt out the Consociation by name. You just didn't. My lips pursed. The FBI hadn't recruited me, but some mysterious section of the Consociation had — which cleared up the inclusion of the vampire and merfolk on the team. A multi-species team for a multi-species shadow government.

"The Consociation," Marie said. She smiled at my reaction. "We're well warded here. Our official title is the Department of Realm Containment. Paperwork puts us in a division called DRC in the FBI. A slew of other acronyms are used in other countries in the Americas." Her thin fingers reached out to shake my hand. "We call it Pyre's Pups."

It seemed a bit arrogant to name a team after yourself. I reached out and took her hand. A liquid gold realm undulated under her, covering the couch and curving away from my thigh by a mere inch. Air lodged in my throat. I recognized the Salmhalla realm by description only; forbidden to humans, it was the home of the dragons. My eyes wide, I stared at a dragon-shifter, or at least whatever part of her dragon form she pressed through into Earth's realm.

Marie nodded, let go of my hand, and leaned back into the red cushions. "You should have some questions. *Some* of them I can answer."

I couldn't speak, let alone form a question. No witch that I knew of, or their immediate ancestors, had ever met a dragon. There were stories, but not in these times. Nowadays, dragons were known only in connection to the Consociation. Unlike any others from outside of Earth, dragons could exist simultaneously in two realms. In ancient history, they were man's introduction to the other realms.

She wanted me to ask her questions. A dragon in Georgia. A multi-species team. To investigate what? My brain spun like a yard full of colorful metal windmills with flashes of thoughts. The air felt hot and dry and my suit and tie suffocating.

Marie gave up on waiting for me to speak. "Okay. We handle the most dangerous cases. Usually crap out of Tarus or some ancient artifact that a hobbyist finds with his metal detector. The last four demons were summoned out of Tarus by high school kids. The ritual had been digitized and hit the internet. Tomas tracked down the data and purged it. We took care of the rest."

I didn't ask who Tomas was. This wasn't a career opportunity; this was a disaster. The witch Finn had appeared calm despite the type of crime the team dealt with. My own abilities did not come anywhere near dealing with demons. I'd been unable to sleep after I'd taken down the crazed werewolf. Four? I hadn't imagined those kinds of things happened enough to require an entire team. Someone would have to deal with it, I supposed.

Marie studied me, and I straightened, wiping what

expression I could from my face. They'd made a mistake. I could whip up a spell from a realm faster than most, but I had no idea how to deal with a demon.

I forced myself to loosen my grip on my purse. "I don't have any experience with all this. Surely you have someone with more training. I'm not that person. I mean — I want to be, but why me?"

"No one is practiced until they are. You made detective at thirty-one. Lead by thirty-three. You faced down a drug-crazed werewolf single-handedly — without letting one mundane catch on. You held three bindings at once on it. If I understand the report correctly."

I jumped when an orange tabby rubbed against her leg. The office had no litter or water. Perhaps that was why there was a hint of incense.

Marie absently stroked the cat's forehead. "Tiberius. He's from a litter of one of my daughter's guests."

"I . . ." My mouth hung open as I had nothing to say. I'd told her I didn't fit in here and Marie had ignored my comment.

She shrugged. "Consider this probationary, on both sides. I obviously believe you have what it takes. Give it a couple of cases to decide whether you agree." Her tone didn't make her suggestion optional.

A moment passed, and I didn't say no. My brain had turned to molasses. On the front lawn of my mind, a color demon windmill spun its arms lazily.

"Good." Marie had taken my numbed silence as agreement. "You'll have a lot to read up on. These incidents are kept not only from the mundanes, but witches and others as well."

A four-person team could only deal with so many demons and other such. Case files would give me a better sense of frequency and what I'd be expected to do. My buzzing thoughts calmed. I was actually considering the position. Her offer to bail after a couple cases eased some of my tension.

"Tomas maintains the original archives. How are you with Microsoft Office?" Marie asked.

"I Excel." The pun dropped out of my lips and I froze. My ears burned and I couldn't swallow past the lump. My grip tightened on my purse.

"Excellent," Marie responded.

The iteration and her tone did nothing to ease my embarrassment. I could only hope that she hadn't noticed my stupid dad joke. Standing as if to run from my blunder, I wondered if we were done.

"Finn is your direct supervisor — Supervisory Special Agent or SSA when we're here in the FBI. He can get you access to everything." Marie stood and offered me her hand again while Tiberius flicked his tail at the lack of attention. "Welcome to Pyre's Pups."

As our skin touched, the liquid gold realm of Salmhalla pooled at her feet. I stuttered. "Thank you—" flushing at her peering gaze, I released her hand and let the realm fade away "—for the opportunity."

I fumbled with the doorknob and didn't breathe until I exited into the outer office. Finn had returned to his desk and swung his dreads as he turned to peer at me. "So are you in?" he asked.

David stood smirking in the middle of the room.

My lips moved, but I just managed a nod of my head.

Finn stood. "Fabulous." He picked up a folder and used it to point to the desk at the front. "I've got logins for our system in here and two more forms I'll need filled out. I had Tomas set you up in the system, so you'll have access to our known entities and objects database. You'll want to get as familiar with those as possible, and the ways we can deal with them."

"The compendium paranormal." David grinned at his quip.

I hadn't moved from in front of Marie's door. My left hand shook slightly as I accepted the folder. Finn had a program pulled up on his screen, but I didn't recognize it. The framed photo showed a much younger Finn and a thickly muscled white man with a brown goatee. They both wore black suits, faced each other, and held hands. They'd posed in front of a white flowering tree for their wedding picture.

"Gary, my husband." Finn said. "We've gotten grayer over the years."

"You both look happy." I pressed the folder against my chest. The moment of personal interaction eased some of my tension.

"We are."

David sighed in a mocking tone. "Eternal bliss." His voice darkened. "Doesn't happen."

I stood in a room with another witch and an ageless vampire while a bald dragon lounged in the back office with an orange tabby. The team I'd been recruited into would investigate or hunt cryptids and entities worse than the werewolf who'd nearly killed me. Our group held some sort of connection to the Consociation, the multi-species government that "advised" nations behind the scenes.

Blowing out a breath, I stepped toward my desk with a growing determination. I had an overwhelming sense of foreboding that I pushed aside.

David's smirk followed me as I passed him. The putrid smell of a vampire came from their constant connection to Tarus. They weren't alive, at least not in the same manner as their original human form. Their hearts pumped, but they didn't need air and breathed only to speak, as David did when I passed him. "Cold case files."

A ratty cardboard box sat on my desk crowding the mouse and keyboard. The initiation of my last two positions had been similar. A supposed chore, I looked at these files with interest. I needed a sense of what to expect and what I'd be doing. I'd moved a thousand miles farther away from my daughter for this position, and it had to be worth it. A sad part of me knew that distance was not the gap in our family, and I sought a purpose to fill that hole. If it was this job, then I should know what I was in for.

Laying my folder on the keyboard, I smiled to myself. "Perfect."

CHAPTER
THREE

I slid a case file from the box and brushed dust off the spine. The musty scent had me nearly sneezing. As fat as my thumb, the file had easily caught my eye. Its title intrigued me further. "Jojo's Nightclub Massacre — mass hysteria," had been written neatly in pen on the tab.

David harrumphed behind me, and I gained a small measure of enjoyment from his response. His attempted hazing had been to my benefit. Learning about what to expect in this new team would be a priority.

I placed the file on my worn wood desk, slid one of the side file drawers open, found it empty, and dropped my purse inside. The rolling office chair had the faint odor of perfumed lotion. I had to adjust the height.

David paced behind me at his desk with hard soled shoes that clicked lightly on the floor. Finn typed in short bursts, as if entering queries. I would have preferred to have my back to the wall, but I didn't plan on rearranging furniture at my new job — yet. My last partner had described me as people-pleasing, but I preferred amicable.

The file held an officer's report, and the date referred

to the massacre as happening over three months prior, on New Year's Eve. Twelve of the beatings proved fatal, and the survivors had been hospitalized. I hadn't even heard of the incident on the news or any media. Someone, probably another agency of the Consociation, had kept it quiet, but that seemed impossible considering the families of the victims.

The officer included a comment near the end. "The statements made from conscious survivors indicated remorse at their actions and an unvarying response that they did not understand why they had been so angry. None could explain any direct dispute with anyone involved. One man had been inconsolable, believing he had killed his own girlfriend."

I would have been at a loss considering the details if this had been my case. The following pages were photographs, witness statements, and coroner's reports.

"Nasty one, that was." David had moved to my side silently, and I only jumped slightly.

"What could cause this?" I asked.

"An artifact would be my guess, but we found nothing. Van was sure we had a demon or jinn in the works. He never had a solid lead, though."

"Van?" I asked, then assumed it was the agent I was replacing. "Is that the merfolk who . . ."

"Sat in the very same chair you are and kept that file in his desk. He'd obsess on some of the cold cases." David shrugged. "His case is heading for this box, if Pyre ever releases it."

"Van died?" I sagged inside at the idea that an agent had been killed, and they didn't even know by whom. I'd dig up those details later.

A printer whirred at the front of the room in the right corner. I hadn't noticed it along the line of gray file cabinets. David straightened beside me, and my pulse sped as he strode purposefully toward the noise.

From the back of the room, a phone buzzed and Finn answered. "What do you have, Tomas?"

The sudden, familiar commotion tightened my chest. We had a case. I did not feel ready for it. Old habits kicked into motion. With my right hand, I touched my holster, then stood. I opened the drawer and dug into my purse to get my badge and phone.

David waited as pages spit out of the printer.

"I hoped you'd have a minute to settle in." Finn approached my desk as I pocketed my badge and phone in my jacket. His eyes were on the open cold case folder on my desk. "At least you won't have to play along with David's hazing. Jojo's was a messy one."

I nudged my chin toward David and the printer. "What's the case?"

"Murder in Knoxville. College museum. The reports are vague but disturbing."

A chill seeped down my neck. "Disturbing? How?"

"Children are the only witnesses. They say a corpse killed their teacher."

Marie opened her office door, and her voice carried across the room. "Get in here."

I felt the immediate need to comply. The printer continued kicking pages into David's hands. Finn tilted his head toward the back, and I followed him through the open door into Marie's office. The odd scent of incense remained, but the orange tabby was nowhere to be seen.

Marie's bald scalp moved back to her desk and dropped behind her monitor. There were none of the usual rolling white boards, oversized monitors, or high-tech that I'd become accustomed to.

Finn led the way to the back table, where I glanced at

the screen on Marie's desk. She zoomed in on a gruesome photo: a dead woman spread across a tile floor, torn apart with her entrails coiled in a pool of blood. Her throat had been ripped open, and open eyes stared to the left of the camera.

With little other information, I immediately considered a werewolf, but my recent experience would color any scene. My apprehension faded as my mind engaged. Quickly, I ran through scenarios where children might construe an attacking corpse. I took the chair toward the back of the table, still able to see over Marie's shoulder.

"Wheels up in thirty-five," Marie said without stopping her inspection of the screen.

The printer had stopped, and David's shoes clicked on the floor. Finn's aftershave wafted in the air as he rested an elbow on the table with his thumb on his chin and two fingers on his lips.

David sighed with an exaggerated waggle of the stack of papers. "For the half a tree they killed, there's not much here."

Marie changed screens to other rooms of the museum, as if on a live feed. She tapped a drawer of her desk. "Folders."

Rolling his eyes, David plucked out four folders and slapped the pile on the table between me and Finn. "Fresh Blood should be handling the printer from now on."

Marie rolled around and faced us as David rattled his mints and took a seat. "Kristen or Winters. I didn't let Van call you Bucktooth, David." She grabbed a collated stack. "Heather Norris, white female, aged thirty-three, elementary school teacher. Killed at ten this morning at a Knoxville museum, over forty minutes ago."

We all picked up a packet of papers, but I listened, twisting a curl.

Marie flipped a page. "Security reported the death to the police. Our people intercepted, and the case has been transferred to us. Local FBI have replaced LEOs, and the building is locked down. Police photos have been retrieved, and no CSI or coroner has made it to the body. Witnesses, her class, are being interviewed by two of the local FBI."

I frowned, unsure how the FBI could take a local case without interstate cause. The Consociation had that kind of leverage.

David snorted. "Who won't believe a word."

"It's being recorded." She leafed through the following pages quickly. "Initial witness reports vary between zombie, mummy, and corpse." Marie slapped the papers down, then picked up a folder. "Thoughts?"

"Definitely Tarus origin. Ghoul?" David offered.

"No flesh eating." Marie turned to Finn. "You?"

"A human corpse could have been possessed. Revenant, demon, jinn. They'd have to be released from Tarus, perhaps using an artifact like Cyprian's Key." He lifted his head to study our boss. "Iliodor or a witch can zombify through Tarus magic."

"Iliodor," Marie repeated the name quietly. "Why, though?" Her eyes flicked up to mine, questioning without a word.

She hadn't asked me about Iliodor, but wanted my theories on this all-too-brutal murder. My heart skipped, and I felt like the impostor in the room. I cleared my throat, conscious that Finn listened carefully. "Possession sounds the likeliest. Maybe someone unskilled opened Tarus and let something in?" I remembered the story about the unsuspecting high schoolers who had summoned demons, and it seemed as though I'd repeated her earlier story.

I had no idea about Cyprian's Key or Iliodor and could

easily be missing connections that would be obvious to someone with experience. Frustration twisted my lips. Normally, I'd be well informed before taking on a new position. My knowledge of Tarus came secondhand for the most part. I'd met a few vampires in my life, but never a walking corpse.

Marie leaned back, and I frowned. Her cat was still nowhere to be seen; perhaps it hid behind the couch. The dragon-shifter stroked a single index finger over her eyebrow; her focus glazed past us toward shelves that lined the back wall. "Let's presume possession until we get better information. This isn't Iliodor, unless we find a museum artifact missing, and then we can go there. That would leave us to determine who opened Tarus and what we're going up against. Pack ammo for a demon or jinn. David can handle a revenant if that's what we're dealing with. We might be a couple days unless we get lucky. Go bags." She stood abruptly.

David and Finn's chairs scraped, startling me to pop up with them. I didn't have a go bag; I had a gym bag with week-old sweats. My purse had some makeup, and I could pick up deodorant and other toiletries, hopefully. Papers shuffled, and I slid mine into the last folio.

Marie raised an eyebrow. "No go bag? Don't worry. I'll grab a couple of extra shirts, and we'll stop at a store if we end up staying at a hotel." She reached for her desk. "Move it."

I stumbled at the gruff tone of her last command and made for the door. We were in a hurry, and my gym bag wouldn't be much use. Wearing the boss's shirts hadn't been a plan, but at least we were close in size. I started a mental list for my own go bag with clean panties and a bra.

David and Finn had moved toward the middle of the filing cabinets. Finn's turquoise-striped purple bag draped easily over his shoulder. David pulled out a rolling case, a garment bag with hangers poking out the top, and a duffel — all pitch black. I had my file wedged into the purse over my neck when Marie strode past with a frayed gray backpack slung over one shoulder.

"Wheels up in twenty-two when the pilots arrive and the plane will be readied. We'll arrive almost three hours after the incident, and we have a hostile still on the premises. Hurry, people. Finn, take Kristen with you to get ammo. Check her weapon." Marie opened the door and turned right at the hall.

David tilted his head back as he followed her through the doorway. "Chop-chop."

Finn slapped the filing cabinet closed, jogged to his desk, and pulled a lavender water bottle with a carabiner clip out of a top drawer. "We'll go over a kit bag on the flight."

"Thanks." I'd had coffee downstairs, but now I was parched. "Wait, flight?" By the time we booked a flight and landed, we could drive there, which I would prefer.

I scrambled to keep up with Finn as he headed for the hall. In the hall we turned left, and I glanced the opposite way where the others had gone, catching David's trim figure stepping into the elevator.

"We have an Embraer Phenom 100." He tilted his head toward the hall. "We grabbed it in a seizure." He jogged to the next office.

"Phenom . . . What's that?" I pitched to a halt as he stopped at an unmarked door.

"A light jet." He tapped a code on a keypad beside the door and the unit beeped, flashing green. The seals on the entrance hissed. Finn slid his finger on the frame, touching the Dur-Alf realm so that dark green dust dripped from his hand.

"Warded?" I whispered.

He entered without responding. Lights flicked on when he stepped to the middle of a room about the same size as their office. Steel plates made up the floor, and translucent panels were illuminated from the ceiling. The air hung heavy with the scent of metal, but I could make out vinegar as well.

Metal lockers of various sizes covered every wall except for a small wooden door at the back. I closed the door behind us, and Finn nodded with approval.

Each locker had a tiny keypad. Tapping in numbers, he unlocked a cabinet on the left wall. "We have most of this end of the hall to ourselves, but governments still set up listening equipment. Tomas takes care of them, but we never know. The office or Jeep is the best place to talk." Inside the locker were drawers marked with numbers and letters. Finn slid a black satchel from a tray at the top and dropped it on the ground. He pointed to the holster under my jacket. "What do you carry?"

"Glock 19." With so much information flooding in, I was a bit flustered.

"Good choice." Finn pulled out a drawer and retrieved a magazine of silver-colored 9mms. Deeper inside, a quick beep sounded before a nearly simultaneous click. He tossed the ammo into the waiting satchel and pulled out a second. He stopped at ten, and each time the locker appeared to be counting before it slid another forward in the tray. It only took seconds, but I'd never seen anything like it.

He spoke as he threw the last magazine in the bag. "A Glock 19 is light enough to hold for a minute and holds plenty of rounds. In most cases we're looking to bring down something small anyway. Salt, vinegar, silver, and mercury in each bullet. Not a healthy mix for a human, but it'll stop their magic dead. Werewolves, vampires, and even incorporeal will react."

I nodded as he spoke. A salt spray had been the most I'd carried for defense against magic users. My last coven had made them look like pepper spray containers. One still rolled around the bottom of my purse. Shooting another witch with mercury didn't sit well with me. Perhaps an ankle holster for a backup would be wise so I could keep more traditional ammo.

Finn slapped the locker closed and pointed to the bag as he moved to a taller cabinet at the back of the room. He pulled out a long canvas case with the shape of a rifle. Patting the side, ammo swayed in a pouch. "In case we meet something that's not small." His grin told me he liked his weapons.

He strapped it over his shoulder along with his go bag and nodded for the door. "Let's not keep Pyre waiting."

When we left, Finn ran down the hall, and I barely kept up until he reached the elevator. He wedged us in with four other agents; some of the people peered at us, but no one spoke. I supposed the regular FBI would have some story about Pyre's Pups. I tried not to let the black bag of ammo rattle, but Finn's weapon case didn't leave much to the imagination. The scent of his aftershave had grown strong by the time we reached the ground floor.

He twisted us through nearly empty halls to a back exit where a bearded, stocky guard opened the door as we approached. A black Jeep Cherokee rumbled at the sidewalk of the parking lot. "Behind Pyre," Finn said as he jogged toward the rear passenger door.

The windows were blackout tinted. I skirted around the back and nearly ate it on the asphalt. The temperature in March had risen, and I felt sweat start under my bra. As I opened the door, cool air flooded over me. Putting the ammo at my feet, I swung my purse around and reached for the handle. At five-foot-five, I had to grab onto a lot of things to scramble into the back of the oversized SUV.

David watched with a grin as I seated myself and shut the door.

"Twelve minutes," said Marie before she punched it.

Finn slid the weapon case behind our seat, arranging some of the go bags to his satisfaction. Even as he shifted items he smiled at me. "Seatbelt."

The way we picked up speed, I scraped the door frame looking for the belt while I kept my left hand stretched in front of me. A musty odor that reminded me of Portobello mushrooms grew stronger as David lathered tan cream over his skin. There were methods a vampire could use to go into the sun without getting crispy. I relaxed as the buckle clasped but took short breaths by the window.

Marie brought us to a quick stop with only a light chirp of tires. I shifted to get a view out the windshield of a stop sign.

Finn pushed me back with a bottle of water against my shoulder. "You don't want to watch," he said, wiggling the water for me.

Marie jumped the car back into motion, and I sat back with my water. It tasted warm but not stale; I drank it while I rested against the door, despite some hairy turns. I thought of the case ahead and calmed as my mind drifted through what little I knew. David finished with his skin cream and offered a charming smile. I was waiting for his next prank — perhaps with some anticipation. I'd been in teams so cliquish that I never fit in; Finn and David had both been welcoming, in their own ways.

"Buckle up," he said. "Pyre and I can't die as easily as you two." Two sharp teeth showed with his grin.

I pointed to my seatbelt buckle. "It took me a minute to get it, then it clicked."

Finn snorted. "You didn't."

I shoved the open water bottle into my mouth as heat flushed up my cheeks. Being nervous or relaxed often brought out the worst puns. At the moment, I was both stressed over my ability and assured by the welcoming feeling I got from my new team.

The new job gave me much more to learn than what I'd been prepped for. The recruiter might not even know what the team did. I considered this a training run, like the first time riding in the front seat of a squad car and not daring to touch anything.

The schoolteacher, Heather Norris, deserved us putting this cryptid to rest. No matter how little I knew. I'd catch up; I always did. We came to another tight stop and then shot into a little airport. A small jet taxied toward one of the buildings.

My pulse rose at the sight of the small plane. "Won't we have to explain this to the FBI at the museum?"

"Stacey will take care of that." Marie spoke over her shoulder and sped toward a parking spot. "Grab everything we need for Knoxville." We jerked to a stop.

I capped the water, no longer thirsty. Marie's driving and the strong scents of aftershave and mints already had me queasy. The last thing I needed to do with my new team was get airsick. I peered out. Only one plane waited outside the massive buildings, and it seemed tiny.

"Shotgun," David called out. "I'm not getting stuck in the lavatory this trip."

I checked Finn, but he had unbuckled his seatbelt and faced the window. That better be a joke.

CHAPTER
FOUR

Juggling the partial bottle of water and the bag of ammo, I trailed last in line toward the tiny plane. The odor of exhaust and fuel wafted in the light breeze. Workers in overalls scurried about, but no one gave us more than a passing glance except for one man, who walked to the opening of a bay and studied us.

As Finn climbed the stairs, he stripped the weapon case and go bag off his shoulder. The entry appeared too small as he leaned down to step inside. As I approached, I was relieved to see it was larger than I thought. Once, I'd taken a smaller plane to Nantucket and been sure we would all die.

I paused at the opening. There were four oversized chairs that would have been in first class on a commercial jet. David sat in one, grinning at me. The aisle between the seating wasn't much, but it didn't look as cramped as it had from the outside.

"Ever flown in a small jet?" Finn asked.

I stepped inside. "No, the only small plane I flew in had propellers."

"Pretty smooth overall. The pilots will let us know if we can expect any bumps." Finn took the ammo bag from my hand.

A smaller seat folded up behind Marie's chair. In the rear on the left, a door closed off a section I assumed to be a toilet stall. I waited as Finn stowed our bags, then I took the last comfy chair opposite Marie. Finn sat to my right.

Facing the back of the plane, I fumbled with my seatbelt and glanced out the small window. I wanted to close it, but the others had left their windows open. Fitting in with a new team meant first following their lead, then I could expose my quirks.

The outer door closed with a dull clang, and I jumped. I didn't turn to look, but the air felt suddenly stale. The metal clasp slipped out of my fingers, forcing me to scramble and find it.

David lounged in his chair, peering at me with a handsome grin. "Only about twenty percent of small jet plane accidents incur a human fatality."

"Stow it." Marie clicked her belt and gave him a dour glare. "We've got over an hour before we get to the museum. We need to focus on the case. Tomas already has some of the preliminary statements from the witnesses we need to listen to."

David's head lolled back to stare at the ceiling. "Third graders who don't know the difference between a zombie and a possessed corpse."

"Tomas promises me a video feed of the museum's recording before we touch down. That should clear up that question."

"Then why listen to kids dribble at all?" David asked.

I couldn't say I disagreed with David. Eyewitness statements proved notoriously unreliable.

As Finn answered David's question, he turned to me.

"Sometimes we learn from the emotions conveyed. A demon or jinn possessing a body will often work to convey more terror in everyone, not just its immediate victims. A glance or motion intended to incite fear might be lost on tape, but picked up by a witness. David knows that."

"Just the facts." David quipped in response.

The running engines pitched higher, and I placed my hands on smooth leather, resisting the urge to dig my fingers into the padding. I wanted to ask how many times they'd flown in this jet, as if some past experience of survival would ease my fears. Big airliners bothered me, but never this bad.

The morning had been a whirlwind. My assumptions about my new FBI career had been dashed, and I found myself untrained for what we were about to investigate. I'd left my life, what little there was, and risked alienating myself from my daughter Jade even more than we already were. Any trip to visit her would now require a plane; hopefully something larger.

Finn reached across the aisle and patted my arm. "I mentioned Iliodor because we've been tracking him for thirty years. All the details are in Tomas's archives."

"I never got a chance to—" I froze as the plane jerked into motion.

He continued in a conversational tone. "A quick overview. A hieromonk who defended the people above the aristocracy. Trained under Rasputin. Eventually turned against him. We have evidence that Iliodor stole some of Rasputin's key artifacts. The Tibetan Gyve, at least."

I knew Finn was trying to distract me, and I appreciated it. Still when the jet began racing down the runway and roared to lift off, it took everything not to grab his hand.

"He faded away in New York and off our radar until

about forty some odd years ago. Before my time. Pyre investigated his death, though."

The takeoff was smoother than I expected, more like a larger jet than the little plane I'd flown on.

Finn glanced at their boss, but when she didn't comment, he continued. "None of the artifacts were ever found, and the body had been cremated. During the sixties, disturbing abilities were being taught to witches in communes with a distinct message of rebellion against the US government. By the seventies, we had our first proof that Iliodor was still alive, amassing artifacts, and gaining followers. After I joined, we almost caught him once."

I loosened at the airliner-like ease of ascent. "What does he want?"

"A rebellion. A form of communism with a spiritual core. His manifesto is in the archives."

I smiled at Finn. "Thank you. I'll make sure to read it." I would, but I was thanking him for getting me through my fears.

Marie had remained expressionless throughout the discussion of Iliodor. She picked up her cell phone, adjusted something on the screen, and lifted it to her ear. "Tomas, we're about to level off. What do you have?"

In a few minutes, Marie pulled out the table between us and unfolded a monitor embedded into it. The screen flickered to life as David rose and began rummaging in the back. "There's no wine," he said.

Marie tapped an icon at the bottom of the monitor. "I told them not to stock it."

"I notice there's still beer."

"Which I drink *after* the case, not before. Make me a coffee." Marie adjusted the volume.

"I thought you'd be focused on the case, not beverages." Tomas's voice was pitched rather high.

"We can do both. Play the video, Tomas." Marie shifted in her seat to angle toward the screen.

He swore. "They're loading. Keep your damned panties loose."

The screen flickered, and the image solidified. A decent quality photo of a museum room showed a woman in blue facing a rotting gray corpse. The head of one child was visible in the far-right corner. I mimicked Marie's position. The woman in the video should be turning, trying to escape.

"Loaded," Tomas said.

"Run!" The woman's screaming jolted me as the video began to play. Her arms stretched to her sides, as if she protected the children. Their own screams were dwindling as they ran.

The corpse moved faster than it seemed it should for its awkward gait.

Heather Norris stood her ground, stepping back at the last minute. She should have run.

The corpse eviscerated Heather with measured efficiency. The pauses appeared timed to elicit her fear and shock. The death blow ripped a swath of her neck open from chin to chest, and the corpse stumbled away without watching her body crumple.

My chest tightened as it ambled in the same direction as the children. There was a pause in the video, then we had a new angle where it tottered into a larger room. The children's screams mingled with yelling from louder adults. The dull pandemonium on the audio seemed enough to turn the corpse back into the room with Heather's body. I blew out a breath, realizing I'd been holding it.

Tomas switched views as the corpse staggered back across the Egyptology exhibit to a door in the corner. "No cameras catch it again for a minute before it crosses this intersection." The screen showed a long shot down a hall, a dim intersection, and a lumbering gray shape that passed surprisingly quickly.

I frowned. There were only cameras at the entrances. A view down the longer hall would have been useful.

Tomas's high pitch continued. "Last glimpse." It was an almost identical view except for the top corner of a door on the right side, and the corpse shuffled past the distant junction. "That's it." A map sprang up on the screen with a red arrow overlay. I could see the back hall that bordered the exhibits on the interior and storage rooms on the outer wall. "That leads to a storage room, an electrical closet, and the access to the basement." Red circles appeared at three doors where the hall ended. "I've got programs tracking any movement on the feeds, but your corpse is left with no exit from this point without coming back into view."

"Excellent work, Tomas." Marie rewound the video, shuffling the corpse backward in a manner that would have been humorous in any other circumstance.

"I know. It wasn't that difficult." He sniffed. "I've loaded the audio reports of the witnesses. I'll add them as they come in."

Marie paused the video where the corpse had retreated from the larger room.

"There's something unsettling about seeing the undead up and walking, isn't there?" David placed a coffee on the table between me and Marie, then tilted his head at me and struck a handsome pose.

I didn't jump on the bait. Vampires weren't undead, just not alive with the same mechanics as humans. I retrieved my water and finished it.

"Revenant," Finn said.

Marie sipped her coffee. "I'm inclined to agree."

My expression probably gave me away, though I didn't want to ask how they knew.

Finn leaned toward me and pointed to the moment of the corpse's retreat. "A demon or jinn might have chased into the crowd to create as much panic as possible with no concern for any risk. That's usually what they crave. Unless they have a more calculated cause. A revenant wants to experience the physical and is a little more risk averse. They want to prolong their experience in the Earth realm."

David snorted. "They are nasty little creatures if they've got a body with any muscle mass. They'll rip your head off as soon as look at you. Pyotr never saw it coming."

Marie leaned back and waved David silent. "Tomas. Did anyone come from these back areas? Staff?"

"One. I matched the image with employee records. Edward Moore, a conservation tech."

"Thanks, Tomas." Marie nodded to Finn who typed on his phone.

I listened as they studied the footage, then again as they discussed the interviews. The young shaken voices played out on the recordings as we descended into Knoxville. A terrified parent broke into one session, and the agent cut the recording short, leaving me in the relative silence of the jet. I could only imagine how I would react if Jade had been in that situation. She had her own personal nightmares to deal with, though.

The urge to pee hit me when the jet had assumed a barely noticeable but uncomfortable downward slant. I could wait for the ground. My interest in the walking corpse dimmed in comparison to wanting to know who had let it loose on Earth. Few witches touched Tarus, as the chance of getting caught up in it held a greater probability than touching the Ya Keya realm.

The landing caught me by surprise, jolting me out of my thoughts. I blinked and peered out the window at the tarmac. The late morning sun hid behind a hazy sky, and I added a rain poncho to my mental list for a go bag.

Before we taxied to a stop, Finn jumped up and started retrieving gear. No one else left their seats, so I held onto my purse and waited.

Marie reached forward and offered me something. "Here."

Before I knew what it was, I accepted it automatically. "Thank you." She handed me a small white case with a USB charger jacked into it. I opened it to find what could have been a gray Air Pod for my iPhone.

"We keep in touch. Let everyone know what's going on. Stick together. Tap it if you need privacy."

I barely had it in my ear before we stopped and the group bustled into activity. The pilot opened the door, and cooler air wafted in with the heavy scent of fuel as I lined up last in the aisle. I thanked the man, sparking a soft smile in his otherwise serious expression. They might always be assigned to this plane; I didn't know, but this wasn't the time for introductions. The petroleum smell grew, and Finn led the way to a glass terminal at the edge of the tarmac.

Marie cut through the small building with a terse response to the man at the desk. Our pace increased as we strode through the corridor, past several small rooms to the front where an FBI agent waited with a black SUV. He had the back hatch open before I exited the building.

Marie frowned as she took the front passenger seat. "How long to the scene?"

The agent looked like my FBI recruiter's older brother

with neatly styled black hair and a quick smile. "Eighteen minutes."

With Finn sitting in the middle, the back seat felt claustrophobic. I leaned my head against the window and watched the city pass by.

Knoxville hardly appeared like a city until we crossed the Kentucky river. Tall brick apartments rose where thick woods, fields, and occasional buildings had been for the past ten minutes. Denser traffic slowed the driver as we merged onto a rougher thoroughfare that ducked under old steel bridges. Taller buildings reached for the low, gray clouds, and pedestrians shuffled on sidewalks. A worn feeling hung on people and buildings alike. When a light turned yellow ahead, our driver cut over a lane and took a right.

I recognized the signs of a university as we drove through a neighborhood of well maintained, old brick architecture, lots of parked cars, students hustling across roads, and plaques identifying buildings' names. Like some cities, the university campus sprawled over blocks and blended with the older buildings. We pulled up to the back of the university museum where the parking lot had been barricaded.

As an agent let us through, Marie knocked on her window. "What's going on there?"

Beside a modern building with neat simple lines, bored workers in green shirts waited on the bed of a well-used truck on the grass.

The FBI driver lifted a finger off the wheel and pointed. "There was a craft event on the lawns. Someone left a trailer by the building. The crew wants to remove it, but the SSA has it inside her perimeter. We're waiting on your team before we release anybody or anything."

Marie grunted. "SSA's got it right."

Three more black SUVs parked along the drive that led to a bay door of the museum. I opened the door as soon as we came to a stop to let in fresh air and space.

Two suited agents were talking with a pair of despondent civilians. A girl with long brown hair who appeared older than third grade reminded me of my daughter as she stood with a blank expression beside a sobbing man. He held her hand tight as her soft flesh whitened, but she didn't react. I could feel her emptiness at this distance.

"A witness?" David followed my gaze.

I shook my head, giving myself a moment to swallow past the lump. "Heather's family." Worse than any gore I had ever seen, I hated talking with families.

Marie turned toward the husband and daughter. "I've got them. Finn, get a report from the SSA. I want to know if there have been any gaps in security. Kristen, you're with him. David, me. And keep that mouth shut."

I assumed she meant the last comment for David and barely heard her words. The girl's lifeless eyes stared at the grass. She knew her mother was dead, and she couldn't do anything about it. I'd been in a similar situation, but not under such horrific conditions.

"Kristen?" Finn's tone suggested he'd repeated my name.

"I'm good." I turned and forced a smile. We'd do what little we could for the daughter: find her mother's killer and whoever set it loose.

"Bag in the car."

My face flushed. I needed to focus. Being new to the team didn't mean I could be sloppy. The others had left their go bags inside. Shoving my purse, my default go bag, under the front seat from the back, I patted my curls when I faced him. "Sorry. Vests?"

"They brought some gear for us." Finn pointed to a tall, light brown woman with our driver.

She studied us with a frown as the driver spoke. They talked near the bay door where another SUV had parked. The back hatch stood open, where she easily leaned one hand on the upper lip. Her gray suit caused her to stand out against the brick wall and dumpster behind her.

Finn strode quickly toward her, and I scampered to keep up, not more than a step behind. I wanted to observe rather than participate. Gray clouds hung low over the top of the building, and the air held a hint of rain. Early spring had brought out some sprigs of green in the grass. As we got closer to the real FBI, the reek from the dumpster overpowered everything.

At the far corner of the lot, Marie knelt in front of the daughter with the husband still inconsolable. David stood aside with a female agent. The daughter's hollow eyes lifted to lock on mine.

I almost plowed into Finn when he stopped and introduced us. "SSA Billings. This is Agent Winters. Any difficulty with the cordon?" His voice had an easy friendliness to it, and he offered his hand, leaning slightly forward.

"SSA Ramirez. Issue with maintenance, but they're holding. Museum staff are sequestered out front, including security. None of them are too happy about it. Witnesses have been picked up by their families. Other patrons were quickly interviewed, and we checked their backgrounds before releasing them. We're told the local police didn't let anyone leave once they arrived. Building is locked down, and we have the keys. Is this your whole team?" She gestured to Marie and David with the family.

"Small unit. We'll need you to keep the perimeter until Agent Pyre gives you the clear."

Ramirez shrugged. "Going to rain. I'll get them geared

CHAPTER FOUR • 37

for another couple hours." She seemed ready to say more, but paused, focusing over my shoulder.

I turned to find Marie and David jogging toward us, and I quickly stepped back, making room. After dealing with the family of the deceased, Marie wore a scowl whereas David beamed toward Ramirez.

"We good on perimeter?" Marie asked Finn.

"We'll hold," answered Agent Ramirez. "I'll get a pop-up for the staff."

"Thanks. Vests?" Marie glanced in the back of the SUV. "Good." She started pulling off her jacket and unstrapping her holster. "Gear up."

Finn and I had our jackets removed before David peeled his off in front of Agent Ramirez as if he were a Chippendale. "David McCree. Are you the SSA?"

"Yes, Agent Ramirez." She didn't sound impressed. Though they were nearly the same height, she lowered her head to look him in the eye.

"Excellent placement out here. Cindy says you had the LEOs out and the place locked down in two minutes. I'm impressed."

"Agent Dyer is being kind, but thank you."

Marie shoved a jacket in my arms. "Save it for the laundromat, McCree. Get geared up."

It smelled closer to rain by the time I had a vest on. I strapped on my holster and one of the flashlights Ramirez had brought for us. David, despite continuing to try and charm her, managed to beat me getting dressed and the new ammunition loaded, not that he needed bullets or a Kevlar vest. Pressed inside the protective gear, I could feel my heart racing.

Agent Ramirez let us in a side door, and I trailed at the rear into a brightly lit workroom with a worn metal table in the back. Cardboard boxes lined shelves, and an empty crate sat on the floor by the bay door. Ready or not, I was on a team about to hunt down a corpse that shouldn't be running around killing schoolteachers. The new bullets in my gun might stop it or just expel whatever possessed it. That same ammo would be deadlier to whomever brought the revenant to Earth from Tarus, if they were still here.

Marie faced us and tapped on her headset. "To the body first."

Pulse pounding in my ears, I turned on my comms as she finished. "Then we check that final corridor where it vanished." This close, her voice echoed.

CHAPTER
FIVE

I couldn't imagine that whoever had loosed a revenant on the museum would stick around, but maybe they hadn't been able to get out. The storeroom smelled like oil or grease and maybe some paint. David's shoes made light clicks on the tile as he walked.

It could have been one of the staff who opened Tarus, but they likely wouldn't wait patiently, or impatiently, out front while we investigated. Maybe they thought only the regular FBI were searching. I wouldn't have expected a team like Pyre's Pups existed.

Marie led us quickly down a short hall and through a door that buzzed as we exited into a large exhibit room. It wasn't until we passed through another entry that I recognized the room where the corpse had paused. A quick scan ahead found the Egyptology exhibit and Heather Norris.

I'd seen some brutal deaths in my previous jobs from beatings and stabbings, but this looked more like an accident scene where the bodies are mutilated. Even the werewolf hadn't left its victim this torn up. The stench of viscera hung in the air.

Heather's blue shirt was brown with drying blood. The yellowish pink intestines draped across her thigh and into the congealing puddle. A trio of flies that had already found her buzzed into the air at our arrival.

The dark red pool had crept out far enough to join some of the spatter where the corpse had reached into her stomach. Coagulated dots marked the floor near the first impact. Closer to the exit, a single glob had been stepped on, flattening it to a nearly dried black smudge. I turned to check the floor leading out of the exhibit. The sole of a shoe left a reddish black circle with a gridded pattern; the blood had still been fresh.

"Well, somebody came in and left," I said.

Marie swirled around and peered at the two spots where I pointed. "Tomas, contact Agent Ramirez; she's the SSA here. I want you and your programs downloaded on every cellphone of the staff who were present. They're being held up front."

"And what the hell am I looking for? Images, texts, phone calls?" Tomas's pitch rose as he listed the options.

"In that order," Mare replied. "If someone has a picture of Heather Norris, I want to know everything they did afterward." She grimaced. "Let's hope it wasn't a student or some other visitor."

Heather Norris stared out the exit where her class had escaped. Had that been her last thought, or was it for her daughter? "What was the daughter's name?" I asked.

Marie leaned down to study Heather's body. "Daughter's Brigid. Husband's name is Pedro."

We took barely a minute to search the crime scene before Marie marched us toward the door in the back. We only paused to study wet slick patches that were likely the creature's footsteps. I grimaced at the thought of the still rotting body oozing fluids. In the sand, misshapen footprints led in and out.

Behind a badly hidden door, bright lights lined a corridor that turned, leading to the back of the exhibit. The warmer air in the gray service halls smelled musty.

The first door we came to hung open, leading into a lab that could have been a coroner's office for the equipment. The acrid scent of cleaning supplies and other chemicals wafted out as the three of them entered ahead of me. Pausing at the doorway, the urge to pee returned. I should have forced the issue at the airport.

"The university has a body farm somewhere on the grounds," Finn said.

"And they process them at the museum?" David asked.

I glanced down the halls, half expecting a corpse to come stumbling after us. Finn shrugged as Marie checked the room. According to Tomas, only Edward Moore had come from these back areas. The FBI had him detained with the rest of the staff. If he weren't involved, then whoever released the revenant could still be down here. I rested my hand on my holster.

Marie nodded David toward a seven-foot-high, double-door locker big enough to hold both me and her inside.

David moved with a casual manner uncommon for law enforcement, but he couldn't be killed, at least not easily. Standing too close to the door for my comfort, he tried the handle. "Locked," he said. David rolled his head toward Finn and smiled. "An assist?"

Not moving from the center of the room, Finn slid two fingers across the realm of Mer, exposing it to my view and tugging at blue-green ripples. He formed a spell of unlocking with a pinch and twist; a rivulet of Mer sprang from where he touched. In a flash, the stream shot across the room and splashed into the handle and seam of the cabinet. If a witch hid in there, they would know we were coming. My hand moved off my holster, readying to call a shield off the Dur-Alf realm that could blockade the cabinet.

The door rattled as David opened one side wide. He leaned in, peering between the shelves without caution. My chest tightened. His nose nearly bumped plastic jars of chemicals. The spaces were small, but dwarves were known to use magic. We weren't necessarily looking for a human. Grinning, he had to know I cringed at his foolishness.

"David, stop showing off." Marie shifted as though she too felt uncomfortable with his risky behavior.

He popped open the other side, leaned back to peer in, then crouched down to inspect the bottom. "Nothing."

Marie peered at me as she exited, and she noted my right hand out to my side rather than on my holster. I couldn't tell if she approved or not.

The next room we checked had a locked door as well. We turned on the lights to a small storage area with an organized set of shelves cleanly placed around the walls. Two crates sat on a table in the middle of the room. One had obviously been opened. Clipboards hung from pegs on the shelving units.

After quickly checking the storage room, we passed an intersection a few paces down, and I found a door at the end with one of the cameras above it. My pulse sped, knowing the corpse had walked this same path. Tomas likely monitored our progress. I studied the floor and found wet footprints which had oozed from the corpse. My next footstep drew me closer to the wall, away from its trail.

Finn unlocked two more storage areas before we reached the last intersection where the corpse had disappeared. The plans of the building showed no exit beyond this point. A faint odor of rot clung to the stale air of the corridor. The wet footprints shone on the floor, leading to the stairs.

"David." Marie pointed him to the first room to the side.

He gestured to the footprints and the open door leading into darkness. "We know where it is."

She cocked her bald head, waiting for him to comply. Finn called a ribbon of Mer to unlock the door, and I realized I should be offering to take turns. Repeated interaction with realms drained a witch's energy. What little he'd done so far wouldn't affect him heavily, but his responses might slow when we actually reached the corpse.

As David and Marie entered the room, I tapped Finn's shoulder. "I'll get the next," I said quietly. The comms still picked it up, so I might as well have announced it louder.

Finn flicked his light at the dark opening. His beam lit a brown shape a stair or two down from the entrance. I stiffened and reached to my side, ready to pull at the Dur-Alf realm to bring up a shield. "Pyre," he called quietly from his comms. "I've got something."

"That's a head." I could make out hair, so not our corpse.

Marie popped out of the room and brought out her own light, then took a step forward. "Another body. I don't see blood."

When David came out of the side room, the three of them blocked my view of the doorway. Marie strode to the opening and searched the bottom of the stairwell with her flashlight before leaning down out of my sight. "Unconscious. Breathing. I've got sounds coming from the basement. David, you lead. Finn, lock that last door. Kristen, take the rear."

The sounds of metal groaning echoed up the stairs. My chest tightened. We'd found the corpse.

Finn gripped the crumbling moss-green of the Dur-Alf realm and pushed it to the frame of the door. The plans had shown an electrical room. Dark dust fell as the lock whipped over door and frame. It faded from my sight as he let go. Until he removed it, it would be easier to jackhammer through the wall than go through that door. I felt better that we wouldn't worry about someone creeping down behind us. Finn stepped to follow Marie down the stairs and drew his weapon.

I followed suit, though shone my light on the man crumpled on the stairs. Dressed in gray-green workman's fatigues, he stunk of sweat and cigarette smoke. He could have been the one to open Tarus or an unlucky janitor looking for a quiet hall to take a break. I would have preferred throwing some cuffs on him, unconscious or not, than leave someone behind us that we might not be able to trust.

An old brick wall cornered at the bottom of the steps. David had already turned and swept his light under the stairs. With each tread no more than a plank of wood, I shivered at the idea of something grabbing my ankle. Adding that disturbing thought to the janitor had me nearly crowding Finn.

If I were dealing with an inhabited corpse alone, I'd rely on a binding from the Dur-Alf realm over a gun. From what little I knew of revenants, they supposedly had a difficult time getting out of any entity they possessed. I'd go with David's experience, though, since vampires dealt with the same realm. I paused at the sound of distant metal scraping, then nearly plowed into Finn descending the last step.

The room ran wide and deep with dusty junk. The stench of the corpse hung in stale air along with a sharper smell, possibly urine from animals. Everyone's flashlights scanned the piles of old displays, crates, and what appeared to be a sarcophagus. The sound came from the back of the room to my left.

"Ready a binding," Finn said.

My chest tightened at his voice, but I adjusted the fingers of my left hand and held the flashlight awkwardly. Tugging a crumbling green portion of the coarse, dusty Dur-Alf realm with two fingertips, I nodded to Finn that I was ready. I'd hoped to just observe on this case, but it wasn't a large team.

"Keep an eye on our six as well. There are plenty of places for someone to hide in this mess." Finn hissed out the last word, as if the piles were a personal affront.

I arced my light around and behind us, but nothing moved except the shadows I created. As we neared the corpse, I could hear the metal creaking as the corpse plucked at it. The noise shrieked at points, as if bone scraped along whatever it worked on. David lifted his light high, so the top of a furnace and a brick corner came into view. Normally, I'd be concerned by the light, but the corpse had no eyes. However it perceived, it wouldn't be affected by our flashlights.

A blue panel of metal flapped at the back of the furnace. A skeletal hand plucked at the edge trying to pull it free from a ventilation shaft. Marie had stopped, and Finn led us up to her. I slipped past with him.

The corpse had its back to us. David moved aside, giving me and Finn room. A smaller panel had already been removed and wires and lines ripped apart. Strips of flesh hung from metal and components. As the corpse reached up with a sinewy skeletal hand, I could see one of the fingers had lost a bone, but the creature still strove, unabated. Some agenda drove it to get into the vent.

Finn looked at me and pocketed his flashlight. "On three." He barely whispered, but the comms picked it up.

I swallowed and shoved my flashlight in my vest. Raising my thumb and two fingers up, I waited.

Bobbing his hand slowly, I counted out the three beats with him, then spun my fingers into the dry realm of Dur-Alf and sent a dark shadow of a binding at the corpse.

Perfectly timed, the two misty threads wove across the room directly for the corpse's back. I'd rarely worked in tandem with another witch, and an exhilaration bubbled inside me. The corpse's flesh sagged and tightened with its labor; it appeared to seek an exit, but questions nagged at the edge of my focus.

At the first tendril's touch of our bindings, the revenant leaped from its prying work, spun in the air, and soared toward us. Our magic twisted to find a target and failed.

My excitement caught in my throat at the sight of this eyeless horror. Fresh blood from Heather had dried across its chest and face. Pieces of lips flapped as it moved.

With the mythical speed of a vampire, David snapped forward to intercept. As quickly, something flashed gold around and past me and Finn. My heart raced and my fingers already spun, searching for Dur-Alf to attempt another binding.

The metal tip of a dragon's tail pierced the chest of the corpse. The head and limbs snapped forward with momentum before it came to a dead stop a yard from David's face. The half skeletal arms hung forward though they lacked any control. As David pinched a black shadow from the decayed head with a sharp movement, dark Tarus glittered along the vampire's back.

David drew the revenant out of the corpse like a soiled dish cloth. The glistening gray realm of Tarus hung off the inky form. The Tarus realm circled around vampire and revenant alike to form a threatening gloom which stretched from floor to ceiling. With a snap of his wrist, he threw the black form into Tarus. The realm faded, leaving only the dingy walls of the basement.

Inanimate, the corpse dangled limply from Marie's wrist-thick, golden tail. Her dragon appendage dwindled in size and retracted, letting the soft body slide to the ground with a wet thud. I let out a breath.

"Clean up on aisle three." David gave me a smug look. "Are we calling in the Kuru?" he asked Marie.

"Yes. Finn, can you handle that?"

He nodded, holstered his weapon, and dug for his phone. With a bemused grin, David peered at my hand which I still had raised in the air. I shivered and lowered my arm.

Glancing at Marie, I saw no hint of her tail or other dragon bits. I'd heard of dragon-shifter's abilities to transform or bring components of their true form through the realms. The speed at which she could summon them surprised me. So much had happened in a few short moments, that I tried to compartmentalize all my questions and sound coherent.

"Kuru?" I asked Finn.

David laughed. "Cute little buggers. You won't ever really see them, but when the taco truck parks outside, you'll know they're here on Consociation business."

Marie had moved forward to study the damage to the vent which the revenant had caused. Finn focused on his messaging. I didn't trust David enough to believe any of what he said. The races of the realms were well documented, and I'd never heard of the Kuru. His joke about the taco truck made no sense. We needed to determine if Edward Moore or someone else had brought the revenant here and caused Heather's murder. I pulled out my flashlight and began searching among the junk farther away from the stench of the decaying corpse. If I had been alone, my Dur-Alf binding wouldn't have saved me.

"On their way, Pyre. Just the corpse, right?" Finn brought out his flashlight and joined my search of the room. "The victim's going back to Atlanta?"

Marie sounded distracted. "Correct. Tomas, do you have Herta and Udy in transit?"

His high-pitched curse sounded comedic. "Of course. I'm not one of your dim-witted agents. I can think on my own."

Marie chuckled. "Thanks. ETA?"

Tomas snorted. "I'll check."

Pulling a strand of a spider's web out of my curls, I backed up from one of the tighter crevices between the piles. A life-revealing spell from the Haven realm might have worked to search the basement, if there were fewer of us in the room. Finn would have considered the option as well but hadn't suggested it.

"David, Finn, get the janitor up to Ramirez. Get him medical attention, but don't release him. He's our best suspect at the moment. My gut tells me otherwise, though."

"Got it," Finn stowed his flashlight and headed past me for the door.

"Don't let David dally up there trying to get a phone number from Ramirez. Get back down here and search the room you locked." Marie's tone didn't come off gruff, just commanding.

"You don't have to talk about me like I'm not here," David said in mocking whine.

"No phone numbers. I don't have time to risk another breach with Tarus."

"Yes, Pyre." David jogged past me as he spoke.

"Udy says forty-six minutes, but I'm calculating fifty-three to sixty," Tomas said over the comms.

Pyre sounded amused. "Thanks, Tomas."

David and Finn climbed the stairs, and we could hear huffing through the comms as they lifted the body. Medics should have been brought to the janitor, but I understood Marie's concerns. If the witch were still inside the building, then we could end up with someone else possessed.

A nagging thirst had grown as I dug through the dusty equipment, exacerbating the fact that I still had to pee.

Marie stood near the damaged vent. "First question, just a niggling issue. Why did the revenant not try to get outside from upstairs?"

I frowned at a small rat darting along the base of the wall. "Too much noise and commotion." Not that revenants feared much of anything, but they did have a sense of self-preservation.

"Maybe, but then to reach this dead-end and not go back? Instead, it dug where it could sense fresh air from the outside."

"You think something else bothered it?"

"The corpse was located in the northwest. It worked southwest and south along the back corridors to come through the first unlocked door it approached. It killed Heather and headed to the next room, facing the northwest again."

I tried to picture the layout in my head but had to take her word for granted. "Okay."

"What if someone opened Tarus again, in the northwest corner? The revenant would feel it."

I really didn't have the experience that Marie needed. Revenant behavior hadn't been a big topic among any coven I'd been part of. "And it ran away from that?"

"Winding its way here to the southwest. Trapped — in its perception perhaps."

I shrugged, but she wasn't close enough to see me. We were speaking through the comms, but David and Finn had gone quiet. Tomas would be monitoring. Her assumptions were based on experience, whereas I had none and probably sounded like an idiot. "So we should be looking in the northwest corner of the building."

"That's the second issue. After all this time, do you think they're still here, hiding?"

I didn't. "They were evacuated with the staff and public. We need to interview the staff."

Marie sounded pleased. "ASAP. Let me get upstairs, then you light it up."

Pride tickled my chest at her agreement, but she'd come to the conclusion long before me. Marie had wanted to know if I could work out similar logic. She turned off her light and strode past me for the stairs. I wasn't surprised she suggested I use the Haven realm to detect any life, just that she'd wasted time talking me through her theories.

I killed my flashlight, and as her footsteps reached the top of the stairs, I pinched the airy white realm of Haven. The effort physically weakened me as working with Haven always did. Twisting off a small piece, I flicked the glowing wisp into the middle of the basement. The darkness faded against myriad pinpricks of light. Scores of rats inhabited the piles around me. A nest blossomed white just a single step to my side, and I backed up a stride. Plenty of life inhabited the area, but no humans.

Marie's body appeared as a dim light above and to my right. We needed to get to the staff and possibly hunt down the public who had been released after too quick interviews.

"All clear," I said. Turning for the stairs, I cringed at the thought of seeing Heather's child, Brigid, again. We couldn't comfort the family with what little we had done. Before I faced them again, I at least wanted to talk with Edward Moore.

CHAPTER
SIX

Ignoring the three rats hiding under the steps, I climbed the stairs to Marie. Residue of the Haven magic always lingered, whereas the other realms appeared and disappeared quickly — unless you held onto them. I glanced to where the corpse had fallen, but darkness hid it. Compared to the musty basement with rats and a none too fresh corpse, the air in the upper hall smelled lovely.

Marie studied me as she spoke into her comms. "Finn, David, we're heading out to interview the staff. Finish checking the room Finn locked, then meet us up front."

I pulled another strand of cobweb out of my curls as I waited. We had taken the revenant and corpse out of the situation, but the bigger problem still waited for us.

Finn replied, "Up front; got it, Pyre."

Marie tilted her head for me to follow. "Tomas, any concerns about the staff?"

"I've loaded the eleven on-site names first. No hits. They're mundane." His pitch grew higher as he moved into a faster paced tirade. "I would have alerted you if anything popped up. As I will let you know if any of the off-site staff get flagged." He cursed, punctuating his irate tone. "I've got some consultants and patron names to feed in as well."

I kept my face deadpan, fighting a smile. Tomas seemed intent on insulting anyone he could, and Marie was not excluded.

For a reason I couldn't understand, she just smiled as if he'd told a joke. "Thanks, Tomas."

The utilitarian halls in the back innards of the museum echoed with our footsteps. Still, down the corridor, I heard David's voice. He and Finn approached, growing silent before we met up with them, where we all stopped under a dim bulb. I'd be happy to get outside after our encounter with the revenant in the basement, the rats, and the cobwebs.

Mints in hand, David rattled them at me. I declined his offer.

Finn lifted his hands with a shrug, blocking the hall. "Ramirez is having kittens about holding the janitor here instead of getting him to a hospital."

"She'll get over it." Marie tapped her comms off and jabbed a thumb back down the way she and I had just come. "Hurry up and check that room. I'll need all three of you working the staff. Tomas says they don't show up in any database, but if any of them have been messing with Tarus, the effect might be lingering on them. I'm assuming you got nothing from the janitor."

David shook his head. "Most I got was the contact with the revenant, but a glancing blow at that."

"Will Tichy," Finn said, "the janitor's name."

Marie motioned for room and marched around them. "Get up front when you're finished. It's this Edward Moore

I want to talk to." She tapped her comms live again, and I did the same.

After the first trek through the back halls, I had a sense of the corners and the side corridors which led into the public area. I cringed when Marie led us down the short passageway to the room where Heather had been killed.

The door opened into sand, and we strode quickly to the tile floor. I focused on my feet and the grit grinding under my soles, trying to avoid looking at the shape ahead.

When we approached Heather's body, the scent of her viscera choked me. I forced myself to not turn my eyes away. She deserved to be recognized. I did my job for her — and her family.

In the outer room, the air grew fresher. Arches and doorways led from the main section to other displays. By the time we got to the front lobby, I could breathe deeply.

Abruptly, Marie stopped and scanned the room and front entrance. A couple benches and a counter were the only furniture, while marketing and displays hung on the walls. Two refrigerators offered drinks and ice cream with a sign on the glass doors warning against bringing food inside the museum. Behind the counter, an open door led into an employee area. A hall in the corner to my right had a sign for bathrooms, and I brightened at the opportunity. My hand lifted from my side, about to motion toward the restroom.

Marie gestured toward the front door. "Northeast." Her arm shifted to point to the left. "The lab, or whatever they call it where the corpse came from, is behind those walls."

I dropped my hand and tried to place the rooms in a mental map. "How do you keep this all . . ." I gestured to my own head.

She smiled at me for the first time since our morning

interview and strode for the front door and the staff waiting outside.

I hesitated, glancing at the bathroom.

"Move it." Wind and the scent of rain blustered into the building when she opened the door. The bathroom would have to wait.

Outside, the gray clouds had turned darker, rain misted down with a slight breeze, and an angry clamor came from two white pop-up tents connected to each other over the walkway to the museum.

As we exited, we passed a frustrated FBI agent who stood in a slicker with an umbrella. He glanced at us with a surprised expression. I nodded and smiled. It had been years since I'd been stuck with guarding a scene; it was one of the most boring tasks, until I was promoted to stakeouts.

The tents holding the staff blocked the view to the street except for some bushes and students hurrying past with curious glances toward us.

Dimly, I could hear David and Finn searching the electrical closet.

Marie paused in the wet weather to lean toward me and speak quietly. "Tap shoulders, shake hands. Get a feel for everyone. I'm counting on you being able to see any trace of a realm, Tarus or not."

"Understood." I didn't believe that a witch who could and had opened Tarus would hold a trace for very long. If I were the culprit, I wouldn't wait here, corralled by the FBI. Still, I had to rely on Marie's experience.

"We'll consider more in-depth interviews as needed."

I just wanted out of the rain. "Got it."

Our arrival into the tent brought a quick glance from an FBI agent stationed inside. Then the room quieted, especially a couple closest to us. Heat had built up, and the air had turned stale and musty. I shook rain out of my curls and stayed behind Marie.

There were more than enough chairs, and five of the staff sat. At the far end, two men resumed talking, turning their backs to the rest of us.

Marie produced a handkerchief, patted her bald head, and stepped up to the closest man and woman to shake hands. I had expected her to hunt out Edward Moore first, but without a description this could be him.

She motioned me alongside her. "We'll be part of the team taking statements and getting you out of here. This is Agent Winters."

I offered a brisk smile and shook each of their hands without any reaction. They certainly seemed mundane. When they introduced themselves, I memorized their names.

Finn spoke through the comms. "Pyre, we're clear down here. Heading out to you."

Neither of us responded.

One of the men sitting in a folding chair had noted us and peered in our direction. I tapped Marie as I walked toward him. A handsome man in his late thirties, he had a closely trimmed goatee and smiled nervously as I approached.

"Agent Winters, and you are?" I reached out to shake his hand.

His soft touch brought no hint of realms. "Quinn Jameson. Designer. I set up the exhibits. I didn't see anything. How long will we be here?" He had a meek tone and remained sitting as we shook hands. I doubted he would open Tarus, even if he weren't mundane.

Marie had followed me and offered her hand as well. "Not long, Mr. Jameson. I'm Agent Pyre. We're trying to clear everyone now. Where were you when the children started yelling and the commotion broke out?"

"Setting up the Flynn Creek exhibit. Waiting for Edward and Blake. I heard someone died." He studied the others in the tent, as if they were the killers. "A teacher."

I tucked three of the names into a box, labeling it Flynn Creek. Marie had made it clear we were focused on arcane magic users. However, I still wanted to place everybody neatly into position. The difficulty came in determining how long before Heather's attack the revenant had been released. I considered asking the designer about time frames with his fellow workers.

A phone dinged from the far end of the tent. A woman in a security guard uniform flipped hers up and glanced at the message.

Tomas spoke on the comms. "Samantha Jeffreys. Security guard. That's your photographer. Her phone should have just alerted her to a nonexistent message."

I imagined the footprint near Heather Norris's body. Tomas had some mad skills to track down someone that quickly. My estimation of his abilities rose.

Marie flashed a smile at the designer, "Thank you."

She took my elbow, leading us to Samantha. Other staff watched us. The woman started as we approached. and she took note of the people focused on us. I wondered how Marie would handle this.

"I'm Agent Pyre; this is Agent Winters. Could we step outside and talk for a moment?"

My eyes dropped to her shoe, then the phone she still held. The group had gone quiet, except for the men in the back, but they whispered.

Samantha fumbled her phone into her pants pocket as she stood. "Yes. Why?"

Marie didn't answer, but walked toward the agent

guarding the tent flap. I followed behind Samantha. A sharp perfume wafted behind her as we followed Marie. Eyes trailed us as we exited the tent.

I winced as the breeze misted my face; the rain had grown to a gusting sprinkle. I'd need something to cover my hair, or I'd have a messy poof for the rest of the investigation.

Marie ignored the rain and took a few steps away from the tent before turning to shake the security guard's hand, opening the opportunity for me to do the same. "A quick question, Ms. Jeffreys."

I sensed no trace of any realm on the woman.

"What did you see when you checked on Ms. Norris's body? Anything out of the ordinary?"

The revenant's corpse had long since left by the time Samantha had taken her picture. The question was a pretext.

"I didn't—"

"We've wiped the image from your phone, Ms. Jeffreys." Marie's expression was patient and otherwise unreadable.

Tomas piped in. "And the text she sent to her cousin. I had more difficulty cleaning that phone, but it ended there."

Marie sighed. "And the text you sent. Please understand that this is an active investigation. Any discussion about what you saw may hinder our progress. I trust you understand the seriousness of the situation?"

"I didn't—" Her face blanched as white as David's, and she chewed at her lip. "I won't mention anything. I do understand." She turned back toward the museum as the front door opened.

Finn exited with a smile despite the weather. He strode slowly as if he enjoyed the rain.

"Wonderful." Marie motioned the woman back toward the tent and waited for Finn.

David stepped through the museum doors and scowled at the weather. He said something to the FBI agent with the umbrella, then David covered his head with his hand and ventured toward us.

Finn smiled at the sight of the security guard scurrying back inside the tent. He'd have been listening over the comms. His dreads beaded with water. My hair would frizz in this weather; I added a simple rain hat to my go bag list.

Marie spoke to Finn. "We spoke to a couple, nothing to be concerned about yet." She gestured to me. "We haven't met Edward, the only member of the staff to come from the back area." Marie turned for the tents. "Tomas, what does Edward look like?"

"In your email. Red-hair. Twenty-eight. Thin build."

David pranced for the tent with a futile hand over his hair. Finn took his time. I tried not to appear as though I'd race David and win.

Marie turned back to us. "Sitting beside the security guard. Both of you check him out. This is just our preliminary round. I need to know if any of them have had contact with a realm."

I followed Marie through the tent flap, and Finn eased in behind me.

Ahead of us, David swiftly strode toward a tall blonde woman in a peach dress. His smile sparked hers as he reached out a hand. "Agent McCree, but please call me David." I doubted a dragon-shifter could sense a different realm other than Salmhalla on people, but David would likely know if there were a trace of Tarus by touch. He tapped off his comms after his introduction.

Samantha stood near another security guard. Perhaps she had mentioned her photo to him; a crime scene picture had a good selling price. On the force we'd spent as much time shooing off would-be paparazzi as investigating.

I searched and found Edward sitting on a black folding chair, curled in on himself, staring at the sidewalk. His demeanor could be suspicious, introverted, or upset over the circumstances. Stepping up to him, I waited as he slowly noted my feet, then glanced up. "Agent Winters." My hand hung in the air without him reaching for it.

Edward tucked his fingers between his legs tighter and shook his head. "When do we get out of here?" I couldn't read him yet.

Finn joined me and reached over to clap the young man on his shoulder. "Agent Billings. Edward Moore?"

In the middle of her introduction, Marie tapped off her comms as she engaged the second security guard.

The young man curled tighter, focused on the sidewalk. He hadn't flinched from the touch. "Eddie."

Finn nodded to me that Eddie was clear from any residue of the realms, then tapped his comms off. I did as well. It helped reduce the murmur in the room.

Just for my own satisfaction, I knelt down as if empathizing and rested my hand on his forearm. "We understand you were in the back when this happened." No hint of any realm came through.

He nodded his head, still not looking up. "Yes. Quinn had me return two stanchions. Me and Blake were helping Quinn set up a Flynn Creek exhibit." Eddie shook his head and snorted. "Did someone really die?"

"Yes." Finn responded, peered at me, and shrugged.

I stood. "Thank you. We'll likely have more questions." I had four of the people placed in boxes, but the timeline still had too much wobble to it.

Turning with Finn toward the back, I nudged my chin at the two men talking together. Marie joined us as we strode toward them. Finn and I started the introductions, checking for any signs of the realms.

One of the men in a gray pinstripe suit, Oscar Phelps, bristled against Marie's interview. "We need access to the museum immediately. Mr. Lynch will be delivering two Tsalagi artifacts that Quinn needs to install. We don't have time for this."

I remembered the dull stare of Brigid, Heather's daughter, and my neck flushed. The lack of empathy and the man's self-importance grated against me. The mother and her family were innocent victims in this horror, and this man cared about an exhibit. I clenched my teeth and kept silent.

Marie just smiled and nodded. "I appreciate your concern. We'll see what we can do." She led us away even as he repeated his demands.

I sighed, pushing down my frustration. Tomas likely was right, and none of these people were capable of opening Tarus without a complicated ritual. Our perpetrator had likely been a patron whom the earlier officers and FBI agents had released. Despite the rain, I wanted to walk the perimeter. By default, I usually checked all windows and exits when I had a new scene. My new team handled things differently.

"When we finish, can we take a loop around the building?" I asked.

Marie nodded. "Good idea."

Finn and I continued our quick pass; none of them had any traces. David hadn't left the blonde by the time we were almost done. Eddie still had my attention, as something tickled my brain when I saw him sitting curled up, staring at the ground. Oscar Phelps glared openly at us whenever I glanced in his direction.

Marie had worked as quickly, and we finished together

by joining David. We worked past him to introduce ourselves and get a read on the woman. She was as clean of the realms as any of the others. I doubted we'd get much more from the museum staff, but a thorough report was needed from each of them.

Marie gestured us toward the exit of the tent. "Take your walk. We've got this now."

The flap whipped from the wind outside, and I realized that walking in the rain wasn't my brightest idea because my hair would be a full-blown mess. Finn led the way, and his dreads shifted across his neck.

I stepped out. The wind had risen. I would have settled for a scarf or bandanna at this point. Those went on my list along with a hair tie.

I shivered and then squirmed. "I really need to hit the bathroom."

Finn laughed and jogged toward the doors of the museum. The agent with the umbrella had it pulled down tight around his shoulders.

Finn's dreads were gleaming from the weather and dripped beads of water onto the entry mat as he held the door for me. I shot past him, nearly slipping on the tile, and raced for the bathroom.

Sitting in the stall, I wondered how many patrons we'd be tracking down. In reality, the first few minutes would have been pandemonium with a third-grade class screaming and racing out the front door. Anyone could have slipped away. I thought of asking Tomas if he had a list compared to those he had on camera, but I wasn't about to turn on my comms now. I'd mention it to Finn. Despite this crash course in their methods, I didn't feel a part of the team yet.

Sighing with relief, I headed out to Finn. "Will Tomas

correlate the people he has on camera leaving with the list the FBI released?"

He chuckled. "I'm glad we're not on comms. We'd get an earful. Yes. That's exactly his kind of gig. He'll have a program running on that.

I started for the front, and Finn pointed back into the museum. "Let's see if Ramirez can get us some slickers." He patted his dreads. "It's getting nasty out there."

The empty museum echoed the occasional squeak of our wet shoes. Someone had dropped a green plastic dinosaur, perhaps a souvenir of their field trip. What would happen to the children? What would they remember?

We reached the back loading area, and my chest hollowed thinking about Heather's daughter and husband. I hoped they'd left by now. As quickly, my anger rose again at the museum man who'd demanded to have the facility reopened. I needed to focus on the facts I had at hand, not my emotions.

Finn pointed to a side room where an agent stood watching an unconscious janitor. We could be risking his life, but I understood why Marie hadn't released him. Despite our assessment, he could be our perpetrator, and opening Tarus at a local hospital could be a disaster.

I had to assume that whoever opened Tarus had some experience, though any mundane could learn to work with realms through specific rituals. Witches had a sense of the realms. It was how they learned. At an early age they could see an interaction with the fabric of a realm, where mundane children had only the slightest sense of it.

Some witches, like my daughter Jade, were so sensitive that they touched realms inadvertently. Other potential witches were never identified. They went through life as mundanes who carefully blocked out what their senses whispered to them. Instinct told me our situation at the museum had been intentional, or at least the interaction with Tarus had been planned, if not the revenant and the consequences.

Outside, the rain dripped off the roof and splashed down gutter drains. Agent Ramirez waited in her car with one of her people. A barricade kept the rest of the lot cordoned off, leaving only the SUV we'd been lent and a Mercedes Benz. My shoulders sagged in relief that I didn't have to see the girl's empty eyes or a sobbing husband. I felt selfish.

"Can we release the janitor to the EMTs?" Agent Ramirez had a stern expression, studying first Finn then me.

"That's on Agent Pyre. She should be with you soon." Finn shook his dreads, sending a light spray of water droplets. "Can we borrow a couple of rain jackets?"

Ramirez tightened her lips and opened the back door, pointing at folded slickers. I guessed her to be more organized than OCD, like Finn. She wouldn't understand Marie's orders or methods.

Bundled in the rain jackets, we headed for the back of the building. Expansive lawns surrounded the museum, and the grass appeared greener with the rain. As we neared the corner, we found that the maintenance workers had disappeared, likely for lunch or just to get out of the rain.

Tossed by the wind, debris blew across the grass on the side. The lawn inclined toward the front. A black trailer angled up to the building. I slipped on the wet ground of the incline but climbed toward the vehicle.

"What side of the building is this, do you know?" I asked, circling the trailer.

"North, maybe northeast."

The long trailer had a lion's head logo on the locked side door. The back had a padlock on it. The sides and rear were unmarked. "Do we know whose trailer this is?" I peered around the grounds, and despite the rain, I could make out evidence of an outdoor event: a random tent stake left with a white cord flapping in the wind, clear plastic from packaging, and divots in the ground hinted at the previous activity.

Finn tapped his comms. "Tomas, do we have a company name for the trailer left beside the museum?"

Tomas swore. "I'll get it."

Scanning the lawn, I peered at a colorful truck parked at the street behind us. Red and green lettering and images marked a catering truck. "Is that a taco truck?" I asked Finn.

He chuckled, but said nothing and left me wondering about David's earlier comments. Who were these Kuru? I'd never know when to believe the vampire. However, someone had to get the corpse out of the public area. People in a taco truck hardly seemed likely, though.

We continued up the slope toward the front of the museum. The corner of the FBI's tent came into view. Marie hadn't contacted us, and couldn't. I tapped on my comms. She and David were likely still interviewing, but they weren't on their comms. I ran through what little we had learned, even from the odd and potentially suspicious Eddie. The staff we had sequestered hadn't opened Tarus.

I faltered on the wet grass and whispered. "Blake. Where's Blake?"

Interrupting my thoughts, Tomas spoke through the comms. "The trailer belongs to Lamb's Lion, Inc., an artist and stage production company out of Athens, Georgia, owned by Fitz Dunn."

I barely listened, waiting to ask a question. "Tomas,

was there a Blake in the eleven staff members you sent to the FBI?" I pursed my lips.

"I sent the list to your emails." Tomas swore. "Didn't check it did you? Any of you?"

I blushed, pulling out my phone; I hadn't even done a head count. Quinn and Eddie had mentioned a Blake, but we never interviewed one. "We need to find out who and where Blake is."

CHAPTER
SEVEN

As Finn picked up speed, I jogged after him toward the pop-up tents. Along the sidewalk by the street, one FBI agent huddled at a barricade. The rain had brought out a fresh scent, but I would rather be dry at this point. My frizz scraped the lining of the flimsy hood.

We burst into the tent, and all eyes turned toward us. Marie left the man she'd been talking to, and Finn led her back outside. I retreated with him reluctantly.

"We're missing a Blake . . ."

"Darcy," Tomas said.

"Blake Darcy."

Marie nodded thoughtfully, then turned and headed back inside.

Eddie appeared frightened as the three of us descended on him. "What?"

"Blake Darcy. Where did he go?"

He shook his head and shrugged, more scared than suspicious.

The rain pattered on the roof of the tent. Everyone had gone silent.

"You and Blake Darcy were helping Quinn. Surely you know where Blake went."

He stuttered, "Sam . . . Sam ran past telling me to go outside."

I glanced at the security guard; she stiffened, but didn't appear too concerned.

"We'll check with Sam. When was the last time you saw Blake?" Marie's voice remained calm.

"Blake wouldn't do something like that." Eddie sounded mortified; there was doubt tainting his tone.

Leaning over Eddie, Marie spoke more forcefully. "Where and when did you last see Blake?"

He dug fingers through his hair as he spoke to the ground. "Heading for the bathroom I think, toward the front lobby. But he'd been in back with me — grabbing two crates. We brought everything out to Quinn."

I had stopped a pace back from Marie.

Finn shifted beside me as a red-faced Oscar Phelps strode to her. "You can't think one of us killed anyone!"

Marie's original tone had been calming; now she cocked her head and spoke firmly. "Oscar Phelps. Archivist. You would know the inventory, correct?"

The red in his face blanched. "You think someone stole something? Blake?"

She pointed to me. "Go with Agents Winters and Billings. They'll escort you back inside. I need to know if you've got anything missing." Marie dismissed him with a flick of her fingers toward me and turned to find our amateur paparazzi. "Ms. Samantha Jeffreys, a word."

Oscar bolted toward me in two quick strides. Worry highlighted the lines on his face. Beads of sweat formed on the large forehead stretching up to a receding hairline. "The Snowden's collection just came in last night. If something is missing from that, we're ruined. There's never been a theft — in my time here." I thought he would push me to get me moving. "If Mr. Lynch hears about this, he'll retract his client's loan."

Finn, a head taller than either me or Oscar, rested a hand on the man's back and led him toward the opening. "We'll check there first. What room was this Snowden collection in?"

The rain gave us a reprieve as we strode toward the museum entrance. The FBI agent studied us silently. I shook the rain jacket when we stepped inside. I hoped we wouldn't have to go past Heather again. The map had shown a number of entrances to the back.

Oscar continued to fret as we walked, and I hung behind them, bringing up my email. Tomas had stated that he'd sent files, but I found nothing from him. I wanted to know more about this Blake Darcy. I found it unlikely that he wasn't in Consociation databases as a witch yet managed to open Tarus. Still, he could have learned one ritual. He should have used at least two, or whatever he summoned could attack him on the spot.

It seemed like overkill, but the revenant and corpse would make a good distraction to get out the front door. It had to be something valuable. I didn't completely buy it, though. I'd been on cases where they'd mundanely gotten away with valuables under tighter security.

Over the comms, Marie questioned the security officer about Blake's whereabouts, but the woman remembered little.

The stench of Heather Norris's viscera had begun to seep into the central room. Oscar babbled on, seeming not to notice. We took a left turn away from the room with Heather's body, and he led us to an employee entrance in the middle of a nature room. A ladder stood open in the middle of a partially completed set, which I guessed to be the Flynn Creek exhibit that Eddie had mentioned.

On the back wall, Oscar unlocked a nearly hidden entry, and as we entered a familiar hall, I glanced up at a camera above the door. By my best orientation in my mind's map of the museum, I believed we were at one of the halls where Tomas had shown the corpse running past.

Something not quite human giggled down the corridor of the intersection.

I paused and opened my mouth to mention what I heard, stopping when Finn gave me a warning glance with a quick shake of his head.

"What was that?" Oscar asked.

Finn swung his dreads. "Rats. We stirred up a couple nests down in the basement."

Oscar blustered, "We don't have rats!" He snorted. "I'll have to change exterminators again."

When we came to the intersection, Oscar led Finn to the left. I peered right in the direction of the basement. Based on Finn's reaction, the sound had to be from something he expected, like these mysterious Kuru. When this case was over, I planned to spend a week in Tomas's database, just trying to catch up on what I'd heard about so far.

Oscar gasped as he reached the storeroom that we'd searched almost an hour ago, the second room after the quasi-coroner's office. "No. This is locked at all times."

Finn didn't let the man know about our earlier search. We'd left the light on. "Check inside, see if anything is missing." He let Oscar rush into the room.

Finn leaned against a door frame and gave me a casual glance.

"Oh my God, oh my God!" Oscar flailed his hands as if trying to dry his fingernails. In my mind, he'd gone from a brutish executive to an angsty teen. "These shouldn't be open."

"What's missing?" Finn stepped forward, peering at two crates on the table.

Oscar shivered. "I'll have to pull everything out." He trembled as he picked one of the many clipboards dangling on racks.

"Okay. Don't leave the room. I'm closing the door." The latch clicked, and Finn put a warning ward from Dur-Alf on the handle. It would alert him but not lock it or cause any damage.

We walked a few steps away, and Finn began updating Marie. The door *had* been locked when we searched it. The entrances were under video surveillance, but Blake would be allowed in these back halls. I couldn't reconcile why Blake would need anything other than a quick spell from Mer to open the lock. Where Finn or I might easily peel the magic off the realm, a mundane could use a ritual to unlock a simple door.

I pointed to the room where Oscar could be heard fretting. "Is that the northeast?"

Finn bobbed his head to the side and shrugged. "Somewhat."

"I don't know much about Tarus magic — does it unlock doors or open walls?" My coven had been highly averse to anything to do with the Ya Keya or Tarus realms. The most information I got was warnings and threats of turning into a werewolf if I even touched Ya Keya.

"Both. Dangerous. You think Blake broke in with a Tarus ritual? Why not use the Mer realm? It would be easier and safer to unlock a door."

"That's what I was thinking." I felt a little more comfortable about my new job when I talked with Finn. I didn't feel as naïve around him.

Marie spoke over the comms. "I'm sending Eddie with one of the agents to help with the inventory. Me and David are going to speak with the janitor. He's awake. Meet us at the Flynn Creek exhibit when Eddie gets there."

I turned to look back the way we came, and a shadow stretched at the corner. Blinking, I leaned forward but only found evenly spaced lights along the ceiling of the corridor and the sharp edge of the intersection.

"What do Kuru look like?" I asked.

A sly grin formed on Finn's face. "The only reliable description we have is taller than a dwarf, long robes with cowls, and fat mittens on their hands. I've never been able to spot one."

Oscar let out a loud groan from the closed room. Finn stepped closer, but didn't open the door.

Eddie's nervous voice sounded from down the hall. I couldn't make out the words.

I lowered my voice. "And they actually drive a taco truck?"

Finn shrugged. "Not mentioned in the description I'm quoting, but we've spotted it several times." He smiled. "The first time we told David about the truck, he pounded on the door demanding a taco."

"Extra rare," David piped in quietly over the comms. "You always miss the best part of that story."

I cringed. I'd forgotten we were on comms. Glaring at Finn accusingly, I remained resolutely silent. Eddie's voice echoed at the corner, complaining about being forced back into the museum.

Marie introduced herself, then David, before she questioned the janitor. "What happened, Mr. Tichy?"

"Don't know. Someone bumped into me. It's fuzzy. I can go back to work. Bum knee is all. A couple of aspirin might help my head." The man had a southern accent and slow speech.

"Did you see who hit you?" Marie spoke in a calm, inquisitive tone. I doubted he'd seen the corpse. If he had, his last concern would be going back to work.

He spoke with a fragmented, confused speech. "One of those whining kids maybe? I didn't see them. Bowled me right over. I think I went down the stairs. I'm okay, though. Quinn wanted me to clean up an exhibit. That class was so loud. I should get over to Quinn's exhibit."

"You're going to rest, Mr. Tichy. I think you're okay, but we're going to have some paramedics give you a look over. Okay?"

The janitor argued a little, but Marie left him with Ramirez. "Meet us at Quinn's exhibit. I've got a plan you won't like."

I assumed she meant Finn, but she might have meant both of us. We remained silent as footsteps echoed from the side corridor ahead.

Eddie turned the corner and faltered at the sight of us. "I thought you said Mr. Phelps needed me?" A wet FBI agent followed the young man.

Finn smiled warmly and opened the door to the storage room. I shifted to see over his shoulder. The crates had been moved to the floor, and the tables were neatly covered with rows of trinkets, which surprisingly had guns and musical instruments among them. In the upper right corner of the room, a camera aimed straight at the doorway.

Oscar clutched a clipboard. "We're ruined," he said.

"Did you find something missing?" Finn asked in a casual voice that appeared to calm Oscar.

"Elvis Presley's ring." His voice shaky and low, just

above a whisper. Then he saw Eddie and his tone spiked. "What is he doing here?"

Finn pulled the FBI agent into view, still dripping from the weather and bearing an unreadable expression. "These two are going to help you identify anything that's missing. Is a ring like this typical for your exhibits?"

"We always have more contemporary displays, considering the students."

His eyebrows rising, Finn motioned to the shelves. "Is the ring cataloged in your system?"

"Just the images which the Snowdens provided. We hadn't gotten a chance . . ." Oscar appeared close to tears.

Tomas's high-pitched comment sounded bored. "I'll dig through their database and pull it up."

Oscar noted that we were turning for the hall and planned on leaving him. He spoke loudly, as if to impress the importance of the loss to us. "It's worth well over one hundred thousand."

Finn nodded. "We're looking for the thief now." He rested his hand on my shoulder, gently directing me to pass the damp agent and head down the hall.

I still found it odd that a simple thief would use Tarus magic, but the value was high. Blake had not been flagged in the system, so perhaps he'd come across an old ritual. He might not know the difference between the Mer realm and Tarus. Just a mundane with dangerous information. It wouldn't have been the first time I'd heard stories like that.

We turned a corner, heading toward the door which led back into the museum's public area, specifically the room housing the display Blake had been working on. "Did you see the camera in the storage room?" I asked.

Finn shook his head. "Tomas?" He opened the door into the museum's public area.

Over the comms, Tomas swore. "I've only got twelve screens. Wait a sec."

Marie and David stood on the partially finished set. Her face had an unusually concerned expression, but David just angled his head and smiled handsomely.

Tomas spoke in short, clipped bursts.

"Okay. The camera is on, but not infrared. Pitch black inside there for hours before and while the revenant enters the museum. Your entry is the first activity."

Marie studied Finn. "So we've got a motive. Money is always better than planned chaos. We've got a suspect. Ramirez dispatched local enforcement to monitor Blake's residence on address. But do you go home after a mess like this?"

Finn scratched at his dreads. "Nope. Bolt hard and fast. Maybe this didn't go off like he planned."

"Or it wasn't Blake," I said. Marie snapped to study me so quickly, I faltered. "Well, he's an employee. He's already got half the access. Why use magic?" The room felt warm with the Kevlar and rain slicker.

"Your theory?" Marie asked.

"Well, I don't have one. It just doesn't add up; a mundane using a ritual to get through a door." I probably shouldn't have said anything yet.

She considered my words for a moment, then nodded. "It's going to work as our lead until you bring me something better. We can likely assume he did not head home, but I'd like to track his movements out of the building and see if we get a sense of how he left and where he might have gone." She flicked her eyes to Finn.

"Agh. That is dangerous," he said. Shifting uncomfortably, he sighed.

"What's dangerous?" I asked.

Finn pointed at a small crate at Marie's feet. "Blake

probably carried that. I've got an old family spell to tap into Ya Keya for tracking."

"Ya Keya is dangerous," I agreed. One wrong touch, and Finn could end up a shifter, a werewolf. "Couldn't we use more conventional means?"

Tomas even sounded concerned. "I've got the kid leaving the back office by the front lobby when the panic hits and everyone starts to evacuate."

Marie tilted her head toward Finn. "Where did he go after that?"

"External security would likely be the university systems. Do you want me to get in there?" Tomas sounded hopeful.

Finn shook his head. "No, Tomas. I'll be careful." He crouched at the crate. The Haven realm lit a misty white as he warded himself with a spell I didn't understand, then he touched the gray fog of the Ya Keya realm. His hands and the wood blurred as if distant or out of focus.

Considered by ancients as the dream world of hunters, Ya Keya's promise of power had trapped many witches into becoming werewolves. As a consequence, they lost some control over their emotions and their physical presence. For me, the biggest drawback was they lost the ability to touch any other realms. Some people vanished, sucked into Ya Keya forever.

Standing slowly, Finn peered about the room, as if seeing something beyond what I could see. His eyes were unfocused, drifting one direction then the next.

Walking in a straight line for the exit, his head swayed. He slowly led us into the central part of the museum. I tried not to want to see what he experienced. No wonder whole covens had been drawn to the Ya Keya in the early ages.

Footsteps clicked on the floor ahead. Directly in front

of us, two men in lab coats strode toward the room where Heather Norris had died. The second man, carrying a satchel, glanced over with a sad expression and nodded. He had pale brown hair on the edge of long, orange sideburns and a lanky build.

The dark-haired man in the lead had a fierce face which never looked in our direction. Since no one called out to them, I assumed one of them was the coroner and the other his assistant.

David and Marie ignored the men. Finn continued his magical search, tracking something none of us could see. His path never wavered, though his head and eyes moved as if the world shifted around him.

Finn turned us into the lobby, then a sharp right to the restroom hall. In his slow pace, he headed for the men's bathroom. Marie followed, but I blushed, hanging back.

David leaned on the wall beside me. "Keep your gun ready."

I frowned at the empty lobby. "Why?"

David nodded toward the bathrooms. "In case Finn loses it and goes all wild and crazy on us."

Closing my eyes, I waited for Finn and Marie. "That was the coroner and his assistant." I doubted anyone else would have been allowed past the FBI.

"*Her* assistant," David corrected. "Herta is a dwarf." He motioned down at his knees. Dwarves were usually just under four feet. He had to be exaggerating.

Had Herta managed the illusion, or her assistant? I had mastered much of the magic from the Mer realm, but my illusions didn't work that well. Not even close.

Finn exited the bathroom, following whatever he saw to the door behind the lobby counter.

The room was larger than it appeared from the lobby. A long white table had chairs which I assumed were for employees. A partial kitchen covered the left back corner. On the left wall was an arch which led into a section with gray lockers. To my right were two more closed doors.

Finn headed straight for the opening and the lockers. I easily kept pace with the group, but kept behind Marie.

Finn stopped in front of one of the lockers and then started to loop back to us. David leaned toward the gray compartment, but Marie gestured for him to follow Finn.

Forming a line, we trailed behind Finn as he slipped behind the counter to the opposite end. We passed the ice cream case and headed for the front exit.

The rain had finally stopped, and the air smelled rinsed and fresh. The agent with the umbrella watched us with only mild interest as we walked left along the perimeter of the building. Our path led toward the abandoned trailer, and I wondered if there were some significance.

We didn't stop, even as Finn squeezed in the small space between the bumper and the brick wall. He led us down the slick grass to the back parking lot. Puddles dotted the asphalt, and Finn plodded through to stop at a space. We waited for a moment.

"Warded," he said. With a grimace, he carefully drew a blurry sigil in the air and yanked his hand back. "He disappears here. Warded by something."

Marie sighed. "Thank you. Tomas, get a make and model on Blake's vehicle, then put out an APB. No contact." She pointed back to the building and the front of the trailer. "What's the story on that?"

"Locked," I said. "Left here after a show. Lamb's Lion, Inc."

"Open it." She motioned to me and Finn. "We'll check on Mr. Phelps, then meet you at the locker. I'm going to release the other staff after Herta clears the scene."

David caught up with her as she strode for the back of the museum.

Tomas came back on the comms. "Blake Darcy has a silver 2008 Toyota Camry. License BBT-4221. APB sent out."

Finn led the way up the slope. The event had covered most of the lawn from the litter of divots and scattered debris. We could hear Marie talking with Agent Ramirez before she cut the comms.

Covering my comms, I asked, "Does she ask you to do that often?"

He shrugged, bouncing his dreads. "More than I like."

I unlocked the rolling door at the back with a twist of Mer and tugged at the Dur-Alf realm to search for wards. Canopies, stuffed animals, display racks, and boxes of posters filled the hot and humid interior. Everything had a musty, hot plastic smell to it.

After searching for a couple minutes, we closed the door, left it unlocked, and headed toward the front of the museum.

Marie's comms came back on as she questioned Oscar, but he hadn't found anything else missing. The man sounded miserable.

Rain dripped off branches by the street and off the edge of the roof. As we came to the top of the hill, we found the FBI agent snacking on a protein bar. I found myself hungry and thirsty at the same time. Working in local law enforcement, we often sent a patrol out to grab coffee and sometimes a snack. I'd grown fond of Belle's cannoli; the café con leche from Pepe's mart always made my day.

We passed the FBI agent and Finn led us back into the museum. We'd chased Blake's trail without success. As we had no direct lead to follow, I sagged, giving in to my hunger and thirst.

Marie spoke over the comms. "Anything unusual?" I thought she might be talking to us, but her comms turned off again.

Finn appeared tired as we headed for the central room. Marie and David came from the direction of the room where Heather had been killed.

"I've got Udy setting up markers to make Ramirez believe we're doing our jobs." With a sense of urgency, Marie barely slowed as she and David strode past us for the back office. "I'm going to want us on the road. Unless we get a hit on Blake's car, I plan to check out his apartment. He's our main focus."

Protein bars and snacks were added to my mental go bag list, which I would have written down if ever paused for more than a second. Our time at the museum had been a dizzy whirlwind. The morning had blown by, and as we moved into the afternoon, there was no sign of slowing down.

The looming threat of more inhabitants of Tarus being let loose on Earth carried an ominous weight and made Marie's haste necessary. I could go hungry until we exhausted our present leads.

Finn had to be tired after working with the realms steadily. I had no idea what energy it took to use Ya Keya as he had. However, he easily turned and kept up with Marie and David. I doubled my pace and still hung behind them.

We wound through the employee area to the alcove, where Marie paused and glanced back at me and Finn.

David passed Marie when she stopped. Finn and I both reached for Dur-Alf to check for wards as David carelessly reached for the unlocked handle.

"David!" Finn called out.

Too late to stop David, I switched to a shield and slid it between the locker and his body.

A dusty green-brown ward blasted off the gray metal surface.

Wind rushed around the room from the Dur-Alf ward. Marie jumped back, and a pink fingertip skittered off the side of my shield to the tile.

CHAPTER
EIGHT

"Night storms, David!" Marie pulled him back and grabbed his arm.

The first finger of his right hand now ended at the middle knuckle, and blood flowed freely. "Yeah, that's going to take a few days to grow back." He didn't sound too concerned.

As I dropped my shield, I scanned the room, then spun to look in the kitchen. A red and white first aid kit had been mounted beside a fire extinguisher at the entrance to the door. I knew little about vampire physiology, but they healed quickly and unnaturally. The amount of blood surprised me.

Finn dug into the moss-green of the Dur-Alf realm and sent a binding to David's finger. I ran for the kit.

The bleeding had nearly stopped by the time I got David to the sink. Ingesting vampire blood could spread their affliction, but general contact had not been reported as dangerous. I pulled on a latex glove out of caution. He smiled as I gingerly wiped off blood. "Don't worry, I'm not letting it hurt."

His hand looked all too human for me to accept that he could control the pain, but he probably could. "I don't suppose we need antibiotics either."

His teeth flashed in a grin. "Bacteria don't like the way I taste. Their loss."

Marie watched with a scowl. "If you were just showing off, you've wasted our time."

"Dumb mistake. I promise. Cross my lips and hope to die." David studied my face as I patted the finger dry with gauze. "You are impressed though, aren't you?"

"Immensely. I had expected your type to be smarter." My lips pursed, wondering if I'd been too crass.

Marie chuckled. "Perfect. Finn, tell the Kuru we need them up here as well now."

No blood showed on the gauze by the time I taped up the nub of his finger. The skin had sealed pink. David gestured to the cuff of his shirt sleeve and jacket where blood had splattered a few drops. "You missed a spot."

Wheels sounded in the lobby, and I turned with concern. Finn shook his head. "It's just Udy, Herta's assistant. They'll take Heather's body."

Marie grumbled about the wasted time and pulled Finn back into the locker room. David reached inside his jacket and tugged out two white gloves of satin or some smooth fabric.

"Might I impose for a further assist?" He offered them to me.

I grunted, but cleaned up and helped him put on both gloves, though it didn't hide the floppy tip of the finger. "Are you going to be okay?" I asked.

"I'll need to regenerate, and that means blood. Care to make a donation?"

I rolled my eyes and started packing up the first aid kit.

"Fangs, but no fangs." Blushing, I whisked up the box and hurried to mount it back by the door.

"Was that a pun?" asked David. He continued when I didn't respond. "It was. And deliciously horrible as well."

My face burned, and I took my time attaching the first aid kit to its holder.

Finn and Marie saved me as they came out. "Nothing," said Marie.

"Except the ward." Finn's tone implied that meant something.

"Maybe Blake retrieved something before he left." I was glad to drop the topic of my pun. "Or, he assumed someone would be investigating and planned to slow us down." I still didn't feel like all the pieces fit properly. Especially if the robbery, or robberies, happened outside of the revenant's timeline.

Marie tapped on her comms. "Tomas, when Herta and Udy clear the building, have Ramirez check with Oscar to see if he needs any more help from the museum staff or FBI. I want this inventory finished today. Top priority. Whomever he doesn't need, Ramirez can release. Then let her secure the inside of the building so she can send some of her people home."

Tomas swore. "I'm a tech, not your damned secretary."

"You're communications. File a complaint if you'd like. I've got to get to Blake Darcy's apartment. Text me the address." Her lips curved, almost to a smile as she tapped off her comms.

As we left and headed for the back of the building, the familiar sound of creaking metal hinted at a body being moved to a gurney. I assumed I'd get to meet the coroner, Herta, and her assistant at another time. Working with a dwarf would be interesting, as they were rumored to be quite brilliant.

Ramirez had left our driver to watch the back entrance, and he released the SUV keys to Marie. We kept the Kevlar as well, and even though the rain had stopped, I kept the slicker just in case.

Tomas reported that he'd tried to trace Blake's phone, but it was offline. Finding Blake would not be easy if he didn't want to be found. I tapped my purse deeper under the seat with my toe and buckled up as the SUV started. The agent had jogged down the drive to shift the barricade for us.

Marie drove as rashly in the downtown traffic, and I stopped looking out of the windshield as Finn had suggested earlier. Instead, I watched the restaurants and drive-thrus we passed. We lurched to starts and stops until she turned onto a faster road with fewer traffic lights. Finn pulled warm water from the back, and I nursed a bottle to try and quench my hunger.

David played with his glove's fingertip, flopping it back and forth with his good hand. "I never got Ramirez's number," he said.

Marie snorted. "I don't believe your charm worked on her."

"Cindy, though!" He shifted his back to his window to face Marie. "Any chance we'll be spending the night here?"

"Not if I can help it."

I patted my curls, hoping I'd be able to go home tonight and deal with my hair. It seemed unlikely, unless the APB gave us a location. Going to his apartment was the next right thing to do, but I doubted we'd get much from it if Blake was on the run.

The buildings along the streets turned from tall brick or sleek concrete hotels and high-rise offices to wooden residential houses with only the occasional corner store. David rattled mints, and their scent hung in the air. When we pulled to a stop behind a parked squad car, I straightened in my seat.

As we stepped out, so did a male uniformed officer. His expression ranged from concerned to obstinate. Another officer exited from the passenger side, but she kept her expression deadpan.

"Agent Pyre. Any activity?" Marie asked the man as he approached.

He cleared his throat and looked away, toward the building as he spoke. "Detectives Willis and Greenville just went in and—"

Marie stepped forward. "Get them out now."

"I—"

She looked at the female officer. "Get them out."

My chest tightened, though Marie's voice carried no panic. Blake had been quite capable in setting wards on his locker and more on his car which kept him from being tracked. Two mundane detectives could stumble into anything.

The woman leaned into their cruiser as the male officer stuttered.

Marie gestured to us and started to jog across the street. A two-story white house, which might have been a stately family residence at one point, had a deep setback from the sidewalk. Its paint and porch in disrepair, it had four mailboxes clustered at the front of the driveway. Two trucks parked on the tan grass. Spindly brush decorated the base of the building. The fresh rain had left beads of water and an earthy scent.

We padded up a damp path leading to the house. "Dancing monkeys," Marie muttered.

No one drew weapons, and I kept a pace behind and to Finn's left. Marie had reached the steps when a scowling woman with light brown hair opened the door. Streaks of gray and lines on her face led me to believe she was in her fifties. A younger man with a brimmed hat followed close behind.

"Detective Greenville. What's the ruckus?" The woman had a harsh voice, but Marie climbed the stairs slowly and confidently as she pulled out her badge.

"SSA Pyre. Our suspect is not to be approached. You should not be investigating. This is our jurisdiction." Marie glanced back at Finn, then stepped closer to the detective and offered her hand.

Detective Greenville took Marie's hand and shook it dismissively. "If we have a murderer in my precinct, we're going to pay attention."

"That's fine. Watch from a distance. We're dealing with a possibly violent suspect. Just don't involve yourself in the investigation. Contact the local bureau for updates."

She moved aside as Finn stepped up, introduced himself, and shook the detectives' hands. They were checking to see if there was any residue of realms on them. As local law enforcement, I understood the curiosity and had sniffed around the edges of a federal investigation myself when I was in their shoes.

Detective Greenville studied us. "How's this involve the FBI?"

Marie glanced at the house as a middle-aged woman peeked out the open door. "Contact our local office for updates." She left the locals to us and flashed a badge at the landlady. "Agent Pyre, FBI. Do you mind if we come inside and talk?"

The woman's drawl clipped over some letters and accentuated others. "About Blake? He didn't do nothing. Good kid. Pays his rent on time." Her yellow-patterned dress draped to her sandaled feet, and I had to remind myself not to place her into some southern, country stereotype.

Finn patted the detectives on the shoulder with a good-natured smile and got them to walk down the steps toward me and David. The landlady still had not relinquished the doorway, so David took three quick steps up to the porch.

"Agent David McCree. Lovely earrings. Can I ask your name?" He smiled so broadly I thought sure his cuspids would show. Instead of showing her his badge, he reached out with his white gloves and held her hand.

She never looked down to notice his missing digit. "Florence." Her eyes never left his.

"Florence, would you mind if we came in for some cold water? I'm parched. It's been a long morning."

She nodded and her lips moved as if to smile before she stepped back. "Blake couldn't have killed that woman like the detective said."

David kept his good hand in hers and led her inside. "Possibly not. But we do need to find him and ask him what he saw at his work."

Finn rolled his eyes as we followed Marie into the house. A thin hall ran beside a similarly sized set of stairs that led up into an unlit space. The worn runner under our feet had been a vibrant purple and red at one point. Everything in the house appeared faded. Even odors of meals past seemed to have seeped into the walls, leaving an indistinct smell.

"I've got lime juice and ice," Florence explained to David ahead of us.

"One of my favorites." David's voice had dropped to a crooning whisper. He led her into the kitchen at the end of the hall to the left and motioned us to the right.

Marie strolled into the combined dining and living room opposite the kitchen and quickly checked the two doors that led from it. One opened into a bathroom and the second to a bedroom, likely Florence's. Marie pointed to the ceiling above, then to me, and then twisted her fingers like the spell I used to detect life.

I nodded and twisted off a tuft of Haven to toss against the ceiling. My energy sagged from using my magic and lack of food. Perhaps David could talk Florence into some cookies. I scanned the ceiling and stopped at a dull prone shape toward the front of the house on the kitchen side. Gesturing to Marie the location, I walked across the hall into the kitchen where the shape grew more distinct.

Florence scowled at my interruption, and Marie peeked in at my shoulder.

"Which room is Blake's?" she asked while motioning to the upstairs.

Shaking juice out of a bottle into a glass, Florence stubbornly resisted, then pointed straight over the kitchen. "He's not here."

Marie stepped next to me. "We know that. Truly we do. He's not answering his phone, though, and we thought maybe something in his room will help us find him so we can talk."

Florence dug ice out of a bin in the freezer, went to the sink as if to run the water, and studied us again. "What happened to your hair?" she asked Marie.

Rubbing across her scalp, Marie smiled. "Hell of a lot easier to take care of than that." She pointed at my hair and I blushed.

I felt a little self-conscious at the chuckle Florence let out, but if it got us into Blake's room, I could handle it.

"Don't need a warrant?" Florence asked.

Marie nodded enthusiastically. "Oh, we could do that, but I'd hate to trouble you and your guests." She shrugged.

"You can let us into just his room as his leaseholder. We don't need to touch anything or bother anyone else."

I stiffened at Marie's outright lie. The Consociation likely couldn't be dragged into court, but I could be held liable. Staring at a brown splatter on the bottom of the woman's avocado-colored fridge, I slackened my startled expression before peering from under my eyebrows.

Florence added water to the glass and handed it to David. She nodded lightly and tilted her head toward the hall before leading the way. I moved out of the way, stepping into Finn.

David followed Florence quickly, sipping at the drink. His eyes shot open wide and his lips puckered. In one step he rearranged his face to its handsome best and crooned, "This is delicious. You have quite the touch with lime juice."

Finn motioned me to follow Marie, and we all headed down the hall and climbed the steps. The way the stairs groaned, I questioned the wisdom of five people on them at once. The upstairs walls were papered in a paisley print with worn spots around the door frames after years of use. An open door exposed an unattractive bathroom with stained tile and a dark shower.

Florence opened the door to Blake's room, and David bowed and swept her in ahead of us. He drank a large swig of the green-tinged yellow drink and rattled the ice like he did mints.

Marie stepped aside, and I touched the crumbling moss-green of the Dur-Alf realm, searching for a pucker to alert me to a ward. I stepped in, maintaining the contact. Considering our experience with Blake, I certainly expected to find something. Finn remained in the hall.

"He's not very neat, but that doesn't mean he's doing anything bad." Florence tugged at Blake's bed covers.

Books and papers had been piled on a small desk, clothes hung off the only chair, and a lump of underwear and laundry were wadded at the foot of the bed. The bureau had a layer of knickknacks with a conspicuous lean toward Celtic jewelry.

Blake had drawn some crude Celtic knots and labeled them with a distinctive flourish to his writing. Blake was more skilled at his letters than his sketches. Continuing to tug at Dur-Alf, I peered at the titles of his books, mostly history.

David smacked his lips. "This lime juice is amazing. I could drink a pitcher. Could I bother you for a bit more?"

Florence tried to glance at us, but David held her eyes with a boyish grin.

"Of course." Her lips tightened. "Don't touch anything."

Marie moved a stack of books as soon as David and Florence's footsteps sounded on the stairs. "Celtic, Old Germanic. Here, Wiccan lore. He's a mundane, studying what arcane magic he can find. Blake didn't ward the room, so there will be nothing here worth hiding. He works someplace else." She shifted the piles, exposing different titles.

I crouched, searching under the bed. Random socks played with the dust bunnies. His laundry was wedged partially under the bed's frame. The cuffs of a pair of jeans had reddish dust coating them. Standing, I dug through the pile with the toe of my shoe and found similar on a second pair of jeans. "Perhaps somewhere with red soil or dust?" There had been yellow sand and grass outside the apartment.

"Good catch." She motioned for me and Finn to head downstairs. She spoke with Tomas as the stairs complained under us. I'd turned my comms off, but could hear her side of the conversation. "He's definitely studying magic. Dig deeper, Tomas. Yes, you can only work with what you have. Deeper. I don't see anything that says Tarus though. Check family and friends where there might be red soil. Iron oxide. He's got a workshop nearby, I'm sure."

David smoothed our way out of Florence's house without me having to try the lime juice. We walked around the building through wet grass, and at Marie's urging, Florence described the property.

"Dad sold everything past that field when I was a kid. Developers, though they never did do nothing." Florence sounded more annoyed about the developers than her father's actions.

"What's back there?" Marie asked. "Any buildings?"

"Not on Dad's property. They all fell down when I was a teenager. We used to drink out there." She gestured vaguely to the west. "When the Andersons sold to the same developers about ten years back, they cleared out their trailers. They left sheds I heard. Blake doesn't dig around in the woods."

Marie circled us around the building to the front, where I studied the new and old residences of the neighborhood.

David bowed lightly. "Thank you for your hospitality, Florence. If we have any more questions, I'll come by and visit."

As he said his goodbyes, I followed Marie, unsure if the landlady had told us everything she knew about Blake. Probably not.

The police cruiser was gone. Marie frowned. "Tomas, check in with county or state enforcement. I want an unmarked car monitoring Blake's apartment."

David rattled mints. "I don't think Blake will be back. He'll get forty or fifty thousand from the ring."

I'd seen suspects do dumber things. "He might not have expected to have to leave like this. Blake could have left something in his apartment that he needs or has a sentimental attachment to. If he's even the one who caused all this."

"Still doesn't feel right to you?" Marie asked.

Florence watched us from just inside the doorway.

We crossed the wet street, and I shook my head. "Maybe he just used the magic because he wanted to test it, but with the access he had, he could have gotten past the door in a dozen mundane ways, including using the Mer realm. It's certainly safer."

"Who then? What's *their* motive?" Marie didn't contest my concerns, but challenged me to explain what would fit if it weren't Blake.

We reached the car, and I faced Marie as she opened the driver's door. "I don't have an answer."

"Keep at it. In the meantime, we look for Blake."

She hadn't dismissed my consternation, and I felt some pride in that. Marie started the car but didn't drive. "Tomas, search the area behind the residence for some sheds southeast of Blake's apartment. I'm hoping there's an old road leading to them, maybe with some red soil."

Tomas swore. "I'm a bit busy. One of the kids caught a video of the corpse. The parents just posted on social media, and the shares are going viral. Give me a second."

CHAPTER NINE

Inside the car, I sipped the last of my warm water. A trace of David's mints hung in the air, and I was hungry enough to consider taking him up on his next offer. His propensity for pranks killed that idea as soon as it hatched.

The car idled, and I assumed we waited for an update from Tomas. I wasn't surprised that a third grader had a cell phone, nor that they were taking videos. Jade had been five when I divorced Anthony, and she had played games on my phone all the time. Two years later, after she'd moved in with Anthony because of my police schedule, he'd bought her a phone so we could keep in touch. I couldn't complain. However, she'd been seven and in first grade.

"Okay. I've got a program tracking it." Tomas spoke after we'd been sitting a little over a minute it seemed. "I doubt the parents are going to give you permission to get into their equipment. Okay to run a pretext link over an FBI email? It'll propagate over their network. I can clean up everything remotely."

"Do it." Marie didn't hesitate.

"I'll slip a BS deep fake into their timeline later, just to divert anyone who's digging." Tomas's tone pitched. "FBI should have taken their damn phones."

"Thanks for taking care of that, Tomas. The area—"

Tomas interrupted Marie. "Ramirez is stating that Oscar Phelps has completed the inventory of the primary storage. He's looking to go to his office. Eddie wants to leave."

"Patch me in to Ramirez."

Our comms rang twice before Agent Ramirez picked up.

"SSA Ramirez, this is Agent Pyre. I'm going to make this more complicated, but I need every storage room inventoried, and the exhibits."

"He's not going to like it." Ramirez's tone led me to believe she wasn't thrilled at the prospect either.

"We've got a murder here, and it's likely linked to stolen items. The more information we have, the closer we'll get to the perpetrator." Marie stared out the window at Florence's apartment house. Her voice never rose in impatience.

"Is this linked to another case outside Tennessee?" Ramirez asked.

Marie turned up and stared at the ceiling, the first sign of her frustration. "Of course," she lied. "Thanks for the assist with Mr. Phelps."

A pause hung in the comms for a few seconds before the connection clicked closed. The inventory had to be confirmed; the man would see that. Marie dropped her gaze to the dashboard. "Tomas. Sheds. Old road. Near us?"

"Yep. I've got the imagery of the sheds you suggested with sections of clay deposits. A development company owns the property and others totaling twelve square miles. The access road to the sheds serves as a driveway through a thin strip of frontage land owned by a Steve Harvey. Two properties east of where you are."

Marie reached for her seatbelt, and I scrambled to beat her.

"It's an old image, but there's four trailers and about a dozen cars on the front property. There's brush on the rest of the road. Can't tell how passable it is."

The SUV lurched as Marie spun the wheel and circled in the road, heading back the way we came. "Thanks, Tomas." Her bald head tilted toward David as she peered down the road.

I didn't relish a hike through wet brush and clay. We passed a house similar to Florence's. I thought about boots for my go bag. Marie pulled into a dirt drive thirty feet past it. Short evergreens blocked the view of the front two trailers, and wooden porches at each side held bikes and folding chairs. A blue pool sagged off to the right, and cars and trucks filled in most of the remaining space. Two children came around the back of the closest trailer to the left and watched us.

Marie drove straight down the muddy road cutting between the residences. Two more trailers rested at random angles behind the front pair, and a semitrailer rusted beyond those. A lanky man with a scraggly beard hopped over the railing of a back porch to our left and ran out to stop us. The words on his gray T-shirt were too faded to read. His expression angry, it turned suspicious as he caught sight of David and Marie's Kevlar vests.

I pointed out a silver Camry parked at the far back beside three rotting sedans with more vegetation than metal visible. Marie rolled down her window and motioned the wary man to approach.

He stayed in front of the SUV, blocking us. "Got no right to be here." I thought Florence had a drawl, but I barely understood this man.

Marie sighed, put the SUV in park, and unclasped her seatbelt. "David, join me?"

"I don't think my dashing good looks are going too far with him, Pyre." Still, David clicked his buckle open.

As she opened the door, the man shifted forward, then back. He might have been on something from his twitchy movements. "Just turn around."

Finn flicked his hand toward his window. A larger man, looking somewhat like a lumberjack close to Finn's size, had exited the double-wide and watched from the porch.

Marie stepped out, her holster visible, and pointed to the rear of the property. "We're just passing through."

"Not without a warrant." The lanky man couldn't stand still but didn't get closer to her.

David's head flicked as he noted the larger man on the porch. "Well—" he spoke loud enough for everyone to hear. He stepped to the front of the SUV and leaned back on the hood. "We can certainly get warrants for a handful of trailers, sheds, trucks, cars, and all the other whatnot you got out here, but that means paying for a dozen agents to spend the afternoon mucking up the place." He lifted a hand up and made a show of pointing to the silver Camry. "However, all we really want to look at is that silver sedan and the woods out back."

The lumberjack took a moment, then strode down the wooden porch with slow thudding steps. He stopped at the stairs and addressed David. "Ain't ours. You're welcome to it." When the lanky tenant started to speak, the big man's hand flicked. "We certainly don't need the Feds spending all that tax money."

David straightened, waving both hands out magnanimously. "I was sure we could come to a reasonable arrangement. We'll make sure to be no trouble to you and yours. Thank you."

Marie stepped to the front of the SUV. "Do you happen to know when the car showed up and who was driving it?"

The lumberjack turned, obviously being dismissive, perhaps because Pyre was a woman or because of her light-brown skin. "Don't know nothing."

The lanky man danced a couple steps nervously. He seemed to be deciding whether to comply with the lumberjack, then sprang back to his trailer.

Marie climbed back in. "Thanks for waving that around, David." Her tone was annoyed. Without buckling up, she sprayed mud from the back of the SUV and drove to the grass where the silver Camry was parked. The license plate matched. "Finn, Kristen, you're up. David, stay the hell away from the warded car."

I groaned quietly as I stepped out and smelled someone's sweet roasting barbecue; I searched, though all I saw were cars, sheds, and the rusted hulk of a semitrailer. Blake's car had been parked in dead grass that reached the door handles. Marie circled around to David's side of the SUV, perhaps to keep him from blowing off more body parts.

Finn and I both tugged on Dur-Alf, and intricate wards lit up on every window. Blake did not intend for anyone to survive getting into his car. I wondered if we were dealing with paranoia or if he had something worth hiding in there. I pulled at the Mer realm, and nothing showed up.

"Clear the car?" Finn asked.

Marie shook her head. "We'll come back to it." She nudged her chin toward the woods. "Let's get back there."

The only sign of a road that remained was a gap in the trees. Brush grew as high as me. Her shoulders straightened with a deep breath. "We'll drive as far as we can. David, pull up a view on your phone." She circled back to her door, and I jogged away from Blake's obscenely warded car.

The grass and bushes smacked and thumped at the bottom of the SUV like they were ripping it to shreds. The sky outside looked no less dour than it had before the rain this morning. I had expected it to clear somewhat, but the threat of a heavier storm appeared more likely. I'd as soon see a blue sky as a meal. My list of items for my go bag merged into a shopping list of snacks that would be included.

Deeper in the woods, the trees had fewer leaves left than I'd thought from a distance. The climbing vines were nothing more than brown twining rope. The brush alternated between dead sticks and hopeful green. Both scraped under us with shrill complaints. A belt in the engine started to whine.

"Okay." Marie said. She put the car in park, and vegetation slapped lightly under the running engine. "We walk from here."

I forced the door open, and wet branches slapped back at me. The lowest ones got closed inside the car. Standing lower than I'd been sitting, I couldn't see much beyond the few steps around me. The rain had brought out the earthy growing scent of the forest.

Marie wormed through the brush to the front. "Finn, you're the tallest. You get lead. Kristen, take up the rear. Keep vigilant everyone. I'm betting little Blake is pretty paranoid."

David shrugged. "I could head out front. It won't matter if he takes a pot shot at me."

Marie pushed him after Finn. "Let's just go as quietly as we can. David, that means no talking."

Even with the ground and plants wet, I didn't think we could make more noise if David did speak, or sing, or yell. Marie was the quietest, and I at least tried. It was a long ten minutes before Finn gestured that he saw something ahead. I had no idea what until another minute later when brown wood formed a roof's peak.

In a few more steps three sheds took shape. One leaned on the verge of collapsing. The second opened to the elements on two ends. The third had a window beside the door with an easy view of our approach. The trees were scant, so the brush grew thick and wild. Blake could be inside watching us, or already hiding outside.

Marie motioned me to her left and pulled away from David so that we fanned out on our approach. Finn pulled his weapon, so I did as well. The thought of putting a mercury-tainted round into a human didn't please me. I'd be getting a backup weapon. We were trained to shoot to kill, but I would prefer not to. Dipping fingers into Dur-Alf, I readied a binding spell but didn't tug it free easily. After all our walking and magic use, I'd burned up a lot of energy, so the quick spell took more effort than I expected.

The shed had a door which Finn could just scrape through and couldn't have been bigger than my bedroom. Hints of pale blue suggested it had once been painted, but the planks were weathered to a sun-bleached gray. Dark gaps the width of fingers had spread between a few of the boards. Finn tugged at Dur-Alf, searching for puckers in the moss-green surface of the realm to warn us of wards. David would see nothing, and I didn't know enough about dragon-shifters to guess Marie's abilities. She let us lead, her weapon drawn but pointed at the ground just behind Finn.

Finn directed me farther to the side of him, and circled his hand in front of his torso, indicating a shield. I dropped the binding and readied that spell, digging two fingers into Dur-Alf and twisting it into shape. After another step, a Dur-Alf lock showed its crusty form along the face of the door and the surrounding frame. I wasn't surprised. However, it was unlikely Blake had locked himself inside. I gestured for David and Marie to keep an eye on our surroundings.

David had circled to the opposite side of the building from me. He raised his eyebrows and smiled when I glanced over, like we were meeting at a bar.

"Blake Darcy? We need you to remove your wards and come out peacefully." Finn looked tired, and he strained as he pulled up a shield from Dur-Alf.

"Let me help," I said. Tugging on Dur-Alf to make sure I didn't wander into a ward, I stepped closer.

Finn nodded. "Last chance, Blake."

I holstered my gun and drew two holds on Dur-Alf. The only way through another witch's lock was brute force; an energy-sucking crushing spell. That tended to make a mess and possibly expend as much force as a triggered ward. Working through the gaps in the wood, I slid a shield in place behind the door inside. The whole building still might fall, but if Blake hid inside, I didn't want to kill him.

Stepping only two paces away, I watched Finn's shield come closer. He'd have to coordinate with my motions. In truth, I could have handled both shields with one hand. Grabbing a fist into Dur-Alf, dust from the realm crumbled out of my clenched fingers. I shoved the wad at the door, and it flowed like sand over the lock. Finn's shield protected us both. With the sound of grating stone, my crushing spell began to compress the door and Blake's

Dur-Alf lock. The wood creaked, barely audible over the two forces of Dur-Alf grinding against each other. My magic would win, but the door would be destroyed.

Marie and David alternated between watching the effects of the crushing spell and scanning the woods around us.

"Blake Darcy, we're coming in. Stand back." Finn dutifully warned our suspect, but like the others, I'd begun to guess he'd evacuated before we'd arrived. The strain of holding Dur-Alf began to wear on me, and Finn didn't look in much better shape. His tall frame sagged forward.

As the lock popped, the wooden door exploded with a roar against the shields. Dust billowed in the air above us. Even as Finn dropped his shield, I kept mine active in case Blake had something nasty planned from inside the shed.

"Runner." Marie sounded annoyed.

She leaped into a quick dash following a lithe form in a dark gray hoodie with an army green backpack. They headed into the woods on the right side of the clearing from the shed. David sped off at an angle with his unnaturally fast gait.

Finn loped behind her, and I dropped Dur-Alf. Pounding my tired, short legs into a full run, I kept up with them, if not a few paces behind.

During my hiatus and move to Atlanta, I'd lapsed on my weekly runs and daily exercise. That would change.

Branches bare of leaves diminished the cover, but the height of the brush around us rose in thick snarls that snagged at my hips. I could easily see the torso and head of everyone but David. I didn't draw my weapon, focused only on keeping our target in sight as I ran.

Blake bobbed oddly around a wide oak tree. He had been heading for it, jumped awkwardly to the left, circled around the side in a wide arc, and then cut behind it.

"Ward," I yelled, grabbing into the Dur-Alf realm.

Closer than me, Finn snapped a binding out of Dur-Alf and threw it at Marie. She stumbled sideways, but her momentum still brought her too close to the tree.

I threw a shield between Marie and the massive trunk. The blast from Blake's ward ripped dead leaves and bark into the air. A raging blast of debris flowed around Marie, bringing her to a stop without rustling her clothes. Neither Finn nor I slowed.

Blake continued to race ahead, just beyond where I thought I might be able to reach with a binding. Lean, young, and fast, he might elude us now that Marie had been brought to a halt.

I considered jettisoning myself forward by pulling some acceleration from Mer, but the two times I'd used it, my knees had given out from the pressure. Finn and I both maintained our pace as we passed Marie, but Blake had almost disappeared into the thin foliage.

David ran into Blake's path before our suspect could react. The vampire moved faster than a human, and our quarry twisted as David grasped an arm.

Blake yelled in pain and tried to draw an arcane sigil in the air, but David grabbed one thumb after the next and raised both hands into the air in what looked like a very awkward position. I released the binding I'd been forming and slowed to a jog behind Finn. Marie's footsteps followed ours.

Drawing in deep breaths, my pulse pounded at my throat. The vest felt hot, and I considered pulling it off. Sweat beaded in my curls. David wasn't taking in deep breaths like me and Finn, but he only needed air to talk. Instead, he smiled proudly, walking a wincing Blake toward us, twisting one hand then the next like a puppeteer.

Blake was in his early twenties with dark brown hair,

unruly from his running. His clean-shaved, youthful face would have given him an innocent look if he weren't snarling between grimaces. Not actually wanting to dig into Dur-Alf any more today, I did anyway and pulled out a loose binding which wrapped him from elbows to fingertips but allowed him to move.

David noticed the new stiffness in his captive's arms and nodded, relocating his grip to Blake's shoulders. "You really need to leave the runners to me, Pyre."

Blake winced and dropped his arms, though I held them in an awkward bind. Elbows together, his forearms stretched ahead of his stomach and his fingers splayed stiff.

She sighed, "David, call it next time." She walked beside me, indifferent to the branches and brush.

David smiled. "I got him." He spoke in mock urgency.

"Before we start running next time." She clapped me on the shoulder, and the gold of the Salmhalla realm pooled around the outer edge of my foot, refusing to touch my shoes.

I paused my slow pace as she removed her hand and the liquid disappeared. Wind rustled the few leaves of the trees around us, threatening to storm.

Marie slowed, studying Blake. "Thanks for the help, whichever one of you did what."

Finn coughed. "I would be the one who threw you off balance. Kristen kept you in one piece."

"Thanks." Marie stopped as David forced Blake to stand in front of her.

His expression rebellious, I doubted we'd get much from him, at least not here in the woods. I needed to understand the team's protocol better.

"How did you open Tarus?" Marie's tone was heavy with a dull ring to it that seemed to silence even the wind in the branches above.

Blake blinked and spoke quickly. "I didn't." He shook his head. "Tarus? I don't touch those rituals."

Marie swore and turned to look at Finn with a smoldering anger. "Night storms." She passed me, heading back toward the shed.

I'd missed something, and my brow furrowed. "What?" I asked Finn.

He shook his head, flicking his eyes at Blake. "Kid didn't do it. He's not the one responsible for opening Tarus." He gave me a long glance but said nothing more.

I assumed we weren't going to speak about his assumption, at least not in front of the suspect. What had Marie done that made Finn believe Blake's answer?

Finn tugged at Dur-Alf, paying attention to Blake's backpack for wards, then he began to unbuckle it from the man. David had to tighten his grip as Blake tried to resist.

"Stay out of there. You have no right. Where's your warrant?" Blake became more frantic as the pack loosened. He sagged when Finn relieved him of the backpack and handed it to me.

Pulling out two flex cuffs, Finn nodded for me to release Blake. The suspect didn't fight as his arms were secured behind his back, nor when Finn clamped his hands together painfully. Blake was no more than a mundane who dabbled with arcane rituals; he had no affinity for the realms. A witch should have needed more restraints to secure him; I'd have to ask Finn about his procedures.

At a glance from Finn, David led Blake toward Marie and the shed. "Come along, little doggie."

Finn stood silently until they were out of earshot. "Pyre can't compel a suspect to answer unless it involves access to Tarus or Salmhalla. Even then, there are caveats in Consociation guidelines."

"Compel?" We all had legends about dragons; some were thought to be able to make humans speak the truth.

Finn nodded. "Answer truthfully even if they don't want to. Blake did not let the revenant onto Earth. Someone else did."

We'd spent the day searching for Blake, and he wasn't to blame. No wonder Marie had been pissed. We were back to square one in the investigation. "And we can't just ask Blake what he was up to? Marie can't. Not like that." My mind spun trying to absorb everything but it was a bit too much new information.

"Yep."

I watched his expression tighten.

CHAPTER
TEN

We'd have to figure out Blake's gig while we looked at the revenant's release with a fresh view.

The energy we'd burned up wore at me. "Well, I need to eat." I flushed at my comment; we'd eventually get a chance.

The wind stirred leaves across the forest floor, promising a storm. Marie stood in front of the small shed, seemingly staring at it.

"Sorry, thinking with my stomach." I gestured to David leading Blake ahead of us. "What do we do with him?"

"If he, a mundane, used rituals for a crime, he'll be interviewed, warned, added to the database, and carefully given to the local enforcement. Regular monitoring will be scheduled." Finn sighed. "Accessing Tarus would have been a completely different matter. There's a special community for that."

"Like a jail, or a 12-step program?" Opening Tarus left Earth open to some nasty entities.

Finn just chuckled. "Blake is up to something. Marie

will want to know what before we leave." He leaned down conspiratorially. "Then we'll mutiny for lunch."

I blushed, but hoped it was true.

Marie turned to study Blake, eyed us, and gestured toward the shed. "You two. Be careful." She put her hand out for Blake's backpack.

I passed off the bag, and as Finn tugged the realms for wards, I kept him shielded. An elaborate ward, a ritually drawn wheel of runes, covered the rotting floor. Triggered, it would bring down the shed. Mundanes could tie realm magic to objects, but they had to use specific symbolism. As a child, I'd learned about the realms using the same rudimentary symbols and words. This one required contact rather than proximity, or even my earlier shielding wouldn't have stopped it from going off when we shattered the locking spell on the door.

Tugging at Dur-Alf, Finn easily disrupted the bindings and rendered it useless. He walked over it and stood at an altar tucked under a gray tarp. Fine dust from the blown door covered everything in the shed. "All clear." As I entered, he lifted the plastic and exposed a chalice and athame, a wreath of dry holly, heavily used candles, laurel, a slate carved with runes into three staves, and a variety of other elements that would not connect with the Tarus realm. "Germanic, Scandinavian. His wards are Dur-Alf. That stave looks drawn for Mer."

"Well, that's a seer call," I said. The runes were specific.

Finn frowned. "Are you sure?"

I'd been studying seers and all the lore connected with Mer for six years. "Yep." My reasons were private, and I hoped he wouldn't push the topic.

"So he was trying to see into the future?"

"Or the past, or divine truth." I studied the altar. "I'm

going to go with divination, though this isn't a set up for that ritual. I'm basing it on elements." I pointed to a number of items including the laurel and residue of wine in the chalice.

Blake's shed otherwise held nothing notable, with most of the remnants of crates in the corners. A stool had dust from the door covering the top; otherwise, it looked newer than the rest of the shed, but well used.

Marie spoke from the door. "Does this help?" She held up a rusted pair of fetters and a key. "Viking according to Oscar. He just confirmed they're missing."

"Off a seaworthy boat?" I asked.

"Docked in Ireland before it sank from a storm. What was he up to?" She spoke loud enough that Blake could hear, and he watched us from under unkempt bangs.

"Divination?" I asked Blake. He looked down, guilty but not willing to discuss it.

David caught my expression. "So, winning lotto so you can hit on chicks in Acapulco? Go for the Riviera; fewer Americans."

Blake shifted and his eyes lit with anger. "Shut up."

"No, no, you're the intellectual type, aren't you? Hit the lotto and retire in your own personal library. Maybe estates in the Hamptons and Bel Air. A little YouTube channel to disperse your meanderings on the inferences of Descartes." David obviously enjoyed prodding the young man, and I frowned.

"You can't understand. This isn't a frivolous whim. I've been searching since . . ." Blake stopped, lifted his head, and forced himself to be silent. Anger lit his eyes.

The searching he'd been doing had been over something deeply personal. I'd guess he'd been adopted, or lost a parent or loved one.

I tapped my comms. "Tomas, what history do you have on Blake Darcy?"

"Already in your email." He dismissed me without effort, either because I was new, or some other bias. Then again, he treated Marie similarly sometimes.

Finn grimaced and sounded chagrined. "Tomas, we never got her set up on our secure email. Never had time, and none of us is in a position to be checking it anyway."

Tomas swore. "Thirty-one-year-old male. You have the address. Barely graduated with an art degree from University of Tennessee. Only child to a Marisa and Ken Darcy, who still live in Claxton. No arrests or priors or major medical issues. No known interest in the occult or craft." He swore again. "Can't Finn read this out to you? He's got a lovely singing voice." The latter comment dripped with sarcasm.

Blake did not look like the happy home life type, nor one to follow rules, and certainly smart enough to get passing grades. "Did you run his face through recognition?" I asked.

"Against the staff and license photos." Tomas trailed off, distracted.

Marie studied me, and I flashed a weak smile. The level of angst and interest in the craft that Blake displayed didn't sound like Tomas's description. I could be wrong. I'd been amazed at what people could hide about themselves.

Tomas cursed words I knew and possibly some from his home realm. "I should have checked his background deeper. Sorry."

My eyes widened. Had Tomas just apologized? Finn shook his head in a warning not to comment.

With a sigh, Tomas continued. "You're with Jack Darcy. Blake's younger cousin. Orphan at eleven. Murder-suicide. Certainly no degree; he got a GED and barely keeps a job. In our damned database since he was thirteen, playing around trying to work seances in foster care and juvie. Gets worse over the years. He's connected to a mundane coven that's three degrees out from Iliodor."

I looked at the grass. Blake — no, Jack — wanted to know about his parents' deaths. At the moment, I hated my new job. We'd hunted Jack Darcy with mercury bullets. A lost son who might never be right. Now he'd spend time in jail for theft, and it would just get worse.

Marie's voice over the comms broke my cynicism. "Tomas, please find a local detective named Greenville. Tell her we've got a collar for some stolen items out of the museum. Give her our coordinates and Jack Darcy's name." Her voice held no anger, or compassion, though I did sense frustration.

Jack glared at the ground with tears in his eyes. My stomach tightened.

Marie stood in front of Jack to speak calmly. "If you decide to use your arcane knowledge to avoid local law enforcement, you drop back into our domain. We'll capture you again, and we don't release, ever. Choose wisely." She gestured for David to bring our captive to the shed. "Zip his legs." Placing the fetter and key back in the backpack, she left it on the ground a few paces from Jack.

I would ask later about our Consociation's procedures for holding criminals. Marie made her threats sound final, and I shivered at a chill.

Marie pulled us out of earshot, watching him. "What do you have, Kristen?"

"Me?" I flushed.

"You said our investigation was wrong. You were right about that. What do you have? I told you to keep at it." She wasn't forceful about her request, but I still felt awkward. I hadn't thought her investigation was wrong, just off.

I cleared my throat and straightened. "The ring. There's a second thief. Darcy probably had the other items, or one of them, in his locker, which is why we don't see him in that room. It's not staff who took the ring — I don't believe."

"So a thief uses the Tarus realm to steal a valuable ring. Motive is there. Your concern is: why Tarus?"

"That's the part that doesn't make sense. Finn or I could get past their security locks, even disable some cameras. It would've been messier, but wouldn't involve Tarus. I don't know anything related to that realm that would make this smoother."

Marie nodded. "Van was our archivist. Mers tend to like research." She paused as if giving Tomas a chance to support her assessment of merfolk. "I'll reach out to see if any of my friends have any tips about using Tarus to get into rooms."

David shook his mints, lifting them ever so slightly toward me. "Iliodor could still be involved somehow. Maybe the fetter and key are artifacts he wants." He smiled. "Or he already handed the King's ring off."

"King?" I didn't reach for the tin of mints.

"Elvis, King of Rock and Roll." David wiggled his hips in a short, whimsical dance.

Marie dismissed him with a wave of her hand. "Showing your age. Keep at it, Kristen." She leaned her bald head forward, waiting for me to continue.

"Worst case. Opened Tarus just for the havoc it would cause. Stole the ring at some point we haven't determined, and wanted to get out in the chaos. It's weak."

"Tomas, we need a complete list of everyone who exited an hour prior or during the chaos. Add them to our list of those released by local enforcement and FBI. Scrub them deep."

Tomas sounded less arrogant. "Already started. I'll have full results in less than two hours."

Marie checked her watch. "First we deal with Greenville, then grab a bite to eat. We'll know when we see Tomas's list if we're booking rooms here in Knoxville."

My smile started at the mention of eating, but faded as I realized my appetite had dwindled while dealing with Jack. I could sense his past tormenting him.

The musty scent of my wet clothes rivaled the cleaner petrichor and cedar of the forest. I leaned against a young oak, unwilling to sit. We might end up in Knoxville for a few days interviewing anyone who had a connection to rituals or craft. That could include mundanes or witches; even vampires and werewolves had jobs or visited museums. Jack Darcy had turned out to be a bad lead, and I wouldn't be able to get close to a reason why someone would use Tarus until later today. I didn't relish spending the night in the hotel without fresh clothes, but I didn't want anyone else hurt, and nothing much waited for me at my new apartment except unpacking.

Detective Greenville stomped into our clearing wearing a raincoat with a hood that didn't hide her scowl. Her partner, Willis, trailed her leading two uniformed officers through the wet brush.

Marie stepped forward and met the angry female detective while motioning Willis and the officers toward Jack. "Thanks for coming out."

Greenville snorted. "Is this your violent suspect? Looks like a college kid."

"He used a fake ID to get a job and infiltrate the museum for purposes of theft. You've got two artifacts to hold him until you run his fingerprints and identify him.

His prints will be in your system." Marie nodded her head once. "You are right that he's not our violent suspect. Book him, hold him, and give us forty-eight hours before you approach the museum staff or search his apartment. It's a clean collar and great press."

"You're looking for someone else? Someone who crossed state lines?" Greenville reacted a little more subdued, but still dug. She'd been given a nice arrest that would put her in a good spot with her department. Still, I didn't expect her to show any gratitude.

Marie didn't answer directly, but handed the detective a card. "When you have any questions for your report, our department will be happy to oblige."

Tomas swore on the comms. "You gave her *my* card, didn't you?"

Marie smiled as Greenville waved the business card and spoke. "We'll be in touch."

CHAPTER
ELEVEN

The storm hit when we were in sight of the car. Finn and I had the FBI rain jackets, and David ran for the SUV. The rest of us jogged through the brush. We were all drenched by the time Marie started the engine with a whirr from something caught inside. The pounding rain on the roof added to the scraping of brush underneath. I sat in a puddle dripping from my jacket.

I could barely see outside, but Marie managed to turn the car around, pass the detectives' car and the squad car, and make it back to the trailer park. When she stopped beside Darcy's car, Finn groaned. "We've got to clear the wards," he said.

Marie looked in the mirror and smiled. "Thanks."

By the time we cleared wards, navigated through the mud of the trailers' drive, and got to a Mexican restaurant, the backside of my pants was wet to the knees. All but Marie had slipped out of their Kevlar during the drive, and I felt chilled. The storm hadn't eased; if anything, the winds had picked up.

We were the sole customers at this time of the afternoon. The decor was a little cheesy and the seats uncomfortable, but the restaurant was open and serving. The scent of spiced beef fought against a staler odor of beer. The young man waiting on us reeked of pot and nervously eyed the FBI rain jacket hanging off my chair. Our holsters didn't warrant a second glance.

Finn and I snacked readily on chips and salsa while we waited for the server to return. My phone on the table, we loaded the secure email app. It let me view but not download Tomas's attachments.

Marie ignored the chips and focused on her phone. "It doesn't look like there were many patrons in the museum except for Heather's class. An older couple and two college women came in separately. No one else since the museum opened this morning. FBI interviewed all but one of the students, Danielle Mackenzie, who had no connections to craft or arcane, nor did any of them show in our database. No prior legal entanglements, except Jack Darcy, who was the only one who booked at the onset." She leaned back and studied me. "What've you got, Kristen?"

Why was she focusing these questions on me? I dripped salsa on my shirt trying to stuff the rest of the chip into my mouth. My appetite had returned during the drive to the restaurant, and I chewed quickly. "We're looking for someone who's mundane. They might already have priors for larceny. This is not the kind of heist you get away with on a one-time or first-time basis. They're only medium skilled at rituals, or they would have built a containment when working with Tarus. We saw no signs of that or ritual markings." I paused at that comment, wondering if we'd missed anything in our search. "Maybe we review the site, looking for something we missed while searching for a person."

Marie had formed a steeple with her fingers as she

listened and nodded crisply. "Agreed. One more pass." She turned to David. "Anything?"

He was watching the young hostess at the front door. "Iliodor or some other strange talisman we haven't found. Finn will have a better theory on that."

Marie sighed. "Agreed. Finn?"

"First theory: the revenant did not originate in the museum; the opening to Tarus came from somewhere else on campus. A thin theory, as I don't know how a revenant presents on digital cameras — I assume not at all. Second, this is Iliodor who orchestrated the two thefts solely to distract us from another. He might have replaced a talisman with a counterfeit like he did in Belgium."

I tried to determine how another crime could have taken place when we couldn't figure out how they stole the ring yet. When I had the opportunity to review Tomas's archives, I would study Iliodor first.

Marie tapped her two index fingers together. "I would say a third robbery is a stretch, and if Iliodor is involved, then he has the ring. It could have been the primary target or the distraction. I can ask Oscar to verify the remaining objects in his latest acquisition. The man's going to have a stroke."

"Does Udy use the Mer realm to create Herta's illusion?" I asked. It was never something I'd perfected more than a shadow in a dark place.

Marie nodded. "You think someone isn't who they said they were?"

"Jack wasn't, but that was mundane." I pulled out one of the last chips from the basket, but hung it in the air. "It couldn't be staff; Finn and I checked them.

David giggled. "The children would be difficult. Parents would have complained about picking up an extra kid."

I pointed my chip at him. "So one of the other visitors. The couple is unlikely unless there were two people masquerading as them. But an interview at their stated residence would bring up any surprises, such as them not being at the museum today."

Marie released her hands. "Tomas, ask Ramirez to do follow up interviews on all four of our museum guests — tomorrow morning." She watched as the server scurried toward them. "That's a dead end if it's true, but I don't see any positive leads."

The man smiled and blinked constantly as he took orders. Marie handed her menu to him. "Two orders of carne asada, well done. No beans or anything with it."

"Rice? Salad?"

Marie didn't sound annoyed when she declined. "No, thank you. Just two orders, meat only."

David handed over his menu. "Same, except raw — rare. Two orders." He flicked his glove, letting the empty index flap.

Finn gestured between David and Marie. "I'll take their salads and a vegetarian burrito. Extra cheese. Side of guac. Side of sour cream."

The server's expression turned apologetic. "The guac costs extra."

Jabbing a finger at Marie, Finn smiled. "A double order then; she's paying."

I ordered a cheese quesadilla and hoped I shouldn't have ordered two. It had taken us a full day to eat. Dinner might not be an option if we were going to search the museum again. I didn't regret my opinion that brought us to that situation, but neither did I believe we would find anything. In the areas where it had counted, we'd been pretty vigilant the first time.

The quesadilla turned out to be a good choice, as they

made it with the sharp cheddar I preferred rather than traditional queso blanco. Their coffee ended up being my favorite, with plenty of whipped cream and a touch of chocolate and cinnamon.

After our late lunch, I took a minute in the bathroom to attempt cleaning the salsa stain out of my shirt and wrangle my hair and makeup into something a bit more presentable. I hurried, thinking they'd be waiting for me, but David took longer.

Finn appeared a bit haggard. He'd used more magic than I had. The tracking through the Ya Keya realm had been two spells prolonged for a few minutes.

"You could grab a coffee to go," I suggested.

He smiled and shook his head. "The sweet tea did the trick, until I can get some sleep. I'll be fine."

David stepped out of the hall from the restrooms and posed, head tilted up. "Gorgeous, am I right?" He did look impossibly handsome. His gaze turned to the hostess. "I'll meet you at the car. I'm going to grab a number." I hoped she was in college at least.

We spent three hours going over the museum. Mr. Lynch arrived during our search, and the locked down museum had him demanding to speak with Oscar. They were allowed to discuss the situation in the lobby privately until Tomas came back with a report that Mr. Lynch was a vampire. The four of us converged on the lobby.

With graying temples, Mr. Lynch appeared older than David, and his eyes were a cold blue. He held a briefcase casually at his side. He treated us with indifference until David introduced himself; I could see the recognition immediately.

Marie stepped to Oscar's side. "I would really prefer that you two continue this conversation tomorrow. I'm SSA

Pyre. Mr. Lynch, everything is quite under control. Would you be able to reschedule with Mr. Phelps tomorrow?"

The vampire glanced at David, then nodded. "Perfectly understandable, SSA Pyre." He emphasized her name, and I wondered if there was recognition there as well.

Marie didn't turn from Mr. Lynch as she spoke. "Mr. Phelps, please let Agent Billings return you to your work. I'd hate for us to run too late into the evening."

Oscar stuttered for a moment, then Mr. Lynch launched a charming smile. "Tomorrow. I'll call in the morning and set something up."

I had been left to witness their conversation, perhaps because I was new. Standing behind and to the left of Marie, I could see the physical similarities between the two vampires. Fit bodies and symmetrical faces, they were innately attractive. As a child, I had been assured that they did not have glamor or a magical ability, but an unnatural control over their features. My eyebrows raised and I prepared to study Mr. Lynch's responses.

When we were alone, Marie spoke. "You know who I am?" she asked.

Mr. Lynch nodded. "I've been in the Americas for a while, Marie Pyre."

Tomas spoke through the comms. "Three hundred and seventy-two years. Mostly in Panama."

"I'm going to ask you a question, Mr. Lynch. Please don't be offended."

He stiffened and a slight frown marred his expression. "Understood."

Marie used the same voice with a dull ring. An odd silence surrounded it. "Did you open Tarus at the museum today or any other day?"

Mr. Lynch stiffened and his lip nearly creased in a snarl. "No, I have not." He looked down, composed himself, and lifted his face wearing a charming smile. "Is your situation here secure? I do not want to risk my client's items. My reputation is paramount."

"Please meet with Mr. Phelps, but feel free to delay the loan until you hear from us." She pulled out one of Tomas's cards, and I stifled a smile. "Call us in about a week if you haven't heard from us."

Mr. Lynch tucked the card inside his suit, nodded to David, ignored me, and headed for the exit.

I waited until he left before speaking. "David, could a vampire emulate another person?" Marie glanced at me, then studied David. I sensed she knew, but left the response for him.

For the first time, I did not like the way David regarded me. He didn't speak immediately and when he did, his tone was ice. "I feel obliged to reveal this information, for the sake of our team and case. I would not want this information to go beyond us."

I held back a shiver, and replied confidently. "I'll consider this confidential and won't discuss with anyone outside of this team."

His expression relaxed to a small degree. "Yes. Given days to adjust, we could rework our physical appearance to look like anyone with a reasonably similar frame. We have learned that it is flawed because the form is betrayed by the tiniest expressions and reactions. Matching a general identification is possible; replacing a friend is not." David sighed, still studying my reaction. "Mr. Lynch did not do this, as it would take over a day to return to a known presence."

A flush of guilt warmed my neck. "Thank you. I'm sorry. It is helpful for us to know that if someone replaced one of the visitors this morning, it might be a vampire we would be looking for."

"Doubtful that a vampire would toy with opening Tarus further." David flashed a smile. "We are ill-loved in that realm, as well."

His last comment closed my throat, and the best I could do was nod. I had little animosity for vampires. The stories had scared me as a child, but as I grew older I learned how they integrated into our society. My largest bias was with anyone who would choose to work with Tarus and lose their humanity.

We headed to meet with Finn. Oscar took thirty minutes to calm down. I had missed a few discussions during the search, so I was surprised when she explained to Oscar that we'd be leaving tonight. She guaranteed him we'd be continuing the investigation and even offered that we might be back, as soon as the next day.

I didn't relish the thought of multiple flights, but I also dearly wanted clean clothes tomorrow. The case had disturbingly stalled. Jack Darcy's choices had ruined his life, but not killed Heather Norris. Unless one of the visitors today had a doppelganger, either vampire, arcane, or witch, then we had no leads. If Agent Ramirez or her people did find an anomaly, then we had a mere shred to work off of.

The storm had passed while we were inside, but the sun had set. Having Marie drive at a breakneck speed down dark, wet, crowded highways had me slink down into my seat, cuddling my purse. I stumbled out of the SUV surprised how much I looked forward to our little jet plane.

CHAPTER
TWELVE

Finn and I put away the weapons and ammo. The funky smell of our wet clothes trailed with us into the empty office. After a day of using magic, I was ready to crash early.

He pointed at the folder he'd given me earlier in the day. "You're going to need to fill out those forms."

I swapped them in my purse with the folder of Heather's case. "First thing when I wake up. What time does everyone get here?"

Finn opened a cabinet, storing his go bag. "I'm here at eight. David comes in around nine."

I nudged my chin toward the back office door. "Marie?"

He chuckled. "Assume she's here."

I slid on my purse and stared at the box on my desk, the cold case file, and untouched computer equipment. "See you at eight."

"You okay?" He shrugged. "With the team and our cases?"

This morning I would have answered differently, but

I'd seen Heather's family, the ruins of her body, and the corpse. We had to stop whoever did this from continuing. Joining the force hadn't been for the pay. Once I saw a threat, I had to try to stop it. I obsessed, and that flaw had highlighted how weak my marriage had been. Jade had been a blessing, but I didn't fit with her dad. The most important thing is family, and I sucked at it.

"Yeah," I said. "I'm good. I'll catch up on the details, but it's important work. I can see that."

He nodded. "Get some sleep."

"It's my dream job." I paused, closed my eyes, then groaned. "Sorry."

Finn chuckled and headed for the door. "I'm going to try and use that one on Gary tonight. Don't expect any credit for it."

"Blame. It's called blame." I followed him out the door.

My blue 1992 Chevy Cavalier waited in a nearly empty parking lot. The air inside was stale, warm, and smelled of a horde of fast food meals steamed into the floorboards and upholstery. It started, so the new battery had kept a charge. The drive from Grand Junction had been rough with the little sedan packed to the gills with my most personal possessions. The trip had turned disastrous in the Missouri side of Kansas City, where only my magic had kept me safe when the battery died.

Pulling out onto Chamblee Tucker Road, I was confident I wouldn't need the map on the phone. I'd selected the two-bedroom apartment primarily because it was less than five minutes from work. I'd only seen this part of Atlanta in the daylight. Except for the style of buildings, it reminded me of Grand Junction. Crime statistics told a different story, but I'd assumed as much considering how populated Atlanta was. I'd grown up in the boondocks of eastern Oregon, but the last decade I'd spent in larger cities.

The apartment complex still had me confused, but after passing my building, I turned around and parked in my space. The stairs curved gracefully up to small landing highlighted with brickwork; the rest of the structure was whitewashed concrete. Climbing the steps to my second-floor apartment, I felt the day in my legs.

The landing was too small but accommodated my entrance and the neighbors with an end unit. When their door opened, I was four steps from the top. My nerves spiked for a second. The stairs suddenly appeared narrow as a tall woman stepped out with an armload of empty cardboard boxes.

"Oh," she said and stopped, peeking around her load. Her short blonde hair had blue and purple streaks dyed into it. Her wrists and elbows were knobby, though she wasn't too thin.

I hurried up the last steps, making way. "Sorry."

"Just surprised me, that's all. Did you just move in too? They had said that apartment was available when I signed. I'm Astrid." She moved to offer a hand, nearly dropped her boxes, and returned her grip to the cardboard.

"Kristen. I just moved in." I had gotten the impression the end units were larger, maybe three bedrooms. Astrid could have a family or roommates. It hadn't been noisy on that wall, not even a television.

"I'm alone." She smiled. "I know. Big place for just me. I like the room."

I found it odd that she'd nearly answered my thoughts. "Me too. Alone that is."

She drew in a sharp breath and nodded. "I'm sure I'll see you then. We can visit once we're settled." Astrid moved to the stairs and started down.

By the time I closed my door, she was heading for the dumpster. Dropping my bag on a stack of boxes in the tiny kitchen, I headed for the fridge to grab a slice of cheese. Hungry more than thirsty, I bit into sharp cheddar while I slid a finger through the rippling Mer realm to grab my glass off the sink. I leaned against the counter, savoring its rich flavor as I levitated the glass to the spout on the fridge door.

The apartment didn't smell bad, just stale and empty. The movers had placed the couch backwards against the wall and then stacked my two end tables inside it. They finished the unusable pile with three plastic bins of clothes on top. From the look of my apartment, the three men who unloaded the moving truck practiced building cairns at rivers.

Water and cheese in hand, I moved to the first bedroom, kicking off shoes and turning on the light with another lifting spell from Mer. The movers had managed to get my bed close enough to a reasonable shape that I'd been able to set it up comfortably. My nightstand was irretrievable under one of the stacked monuments in the living room. I'd tried a small cash bribe to get them to readjust items, but they'd arrived late and wanted to be done for the day.

I carefully balanced my water on a box of art supplies and finished my cheese. Sitting on a soft and welcoming mattress, I peeled off my holster. Checking the window shade for the tenth or twentieth time, I stripped off my clothes and bra and threw on a loose T-shirt. The day had drained my energy, and I was still hungry.

Heading back for more cheese and water, I diverted to grab my phone out of my purse. The mess in my living room had been my plan for tonight. It drove me nuts. Standing in the kitchen, I checked the time, calculated the difference in zones to eastern Oregon, and took a deep breath before calling Jade.

It took four rings before she answered. "Hey, Mom." She wouldn't ask about work; we'd long since danced around that subject, and there was less about this job that I'd be willing to talk about. Besides, she was twelve and we'd reached the stage where I had to ask all the questions. I should have been around more when she was five and all talk.

"Hi, Honey. How are you feeling today?"

She knew where my question was headed. "Good. Nothing spooky."

"Well, what did you do today?" I popped open the fridge quietly, peeling off two slices of cheddar while trying not to rustle the plastic wrapper.

"School."

I paused, back leaning against the fridge with cheese wafting in front of my nose. "Learn anything interesting?" I bit pungent cheese and swore I'd find someplace to get fresh bread. Tomorrow night, after work, I promised myself.

"Nope."

After barely chewing, I hurriedly swallowed down a thick lump. "So, I met some of my coworkers today." I'd have to carry the conversation as much as I could. The gap between me and my daughter was my fault, and I intended to shorten it, even if it meant boring stories. "It rained where we were." I thought about the plane, but I probably shouldn't mention it. Pretty much everything I did today was likely off limits. "It's already pretty warm during the day. Was it cold at home there?"

"Not really." I could hear a television in the background in another room.

"When is summer break?" Leaving my water on the

counter, I strolled back into the bedroom. "I should plan some time off to fly out there."

"I'll find out the dates and text you." Her tone shifted. Perhaps she expected me to know the dates. My ex, Anthony, would have them marked on a calendar in their kitchen.

"Well, do you want me to come out?" I winced, feeling like I was begging or fishing for some connection between us.

"If you can." Jade's tone was flat. How many times had work overridden a planned visit? I couldn't blame her.

"It's the FBI," I lied. "They're probably much better on coverage." I knew that wouldn't be the case. I popped open the top of one of my art boxes. Three unfinished character cards slid across a sketch pad. On one I'd worked out the basic contours of my boss's face from Grand Junction. I'd detailed the wings and tail, part of the border, and done a good job of lettering "Dragon Lady" at the bottom. I almost laughed.

"Mom," Jade said in almost questioning voice, then she followed with a more reticent tone. "I should get back to my homework."

I dropped the card into the box and sagged to sit on the bed. "Okay, Honey. I love you, Jade."

"Me too." She hung up.

I flipped the phone over and placed it on my pants. Moving this far east hadn't made it worse. However many miles away didn't really create the gap. My past behavior did. When she'd been young, it hadn't seemed she needed me as much as my job had. I'd been taught and believed that family came first, but there were criminals out there hurting people. I thought of our case today, and my chest tightened.

I still had to get some of this mess organized, or I'd

start twitching at the sight. Sitting up in the bed, I scooped a bit of the Mer realm with one finger and sent it to tug on the closet door, exposing the jumbled mess inside. I had so much organizing to do. I needed a go bag. Tomorrow might be another flight to Knoxville.

Standing up, I studied my three suitcases still waiting to be unpacked. Wedged against the wall, my backpack, purchased ten years ago from a Supernatural convention, sported their logo. David would never let me live it down.

CHAPTER
THIRTEEN

After attempting to wrangle some order out of my living room, I arrived at work the next morning severely lacking sleep. I suspected I might have had nightmares, but I only woke with the feeling that I'd forgotten something or left it behind. If I could have found and unpacked the kitchen box, I would have had an omelet for breakfast instead of eating cold cheese while I filled out the forms Finn had given me.

Finn sat at his desk wearing a lavender shirt and offered a rested smile. "Morning. You're bright and early."

I wanted to make sure I beat David in so I could store my go bag without comments. "I've got the form filled out and the start of a go bag." Hefting my backpack up, I kept the logo pointed toward me.

"Excellent." He placed a pen on his table, stood, and motioned toward the cabinets. "These aren't real kits like we used in the military. I keep some snacks, toiletries, and a couple changes of clothes." He opened an empty bottom file drawer and I slid my pack inside. "A little first aid is good too."

As he closed the cabinet, I dug in my purse and pulled out the forms. "I'll add to the go bag once I go shopping." I handed him the file folder. "These are all signed. I kept the info page so I can log into the system today." I'd found my email information. "I'm guessing we're waiting for Agent Ramirez before we move on anything." I had the sinking feeling we weren't going to have any leads. Perhaps that had been the dream that left me in a funk.

"Pyre is waiting on that, but she wants us to check in with Herta. The autopsy report is as expected." Finn smiled. "Now's a good chance to get to know her before David wants to join us and gets her all riled up."

I took off my purse and headed for my desk. "Herta doesn't like David?" It didn't surprise me; he could be annoying.

"She doesn't like vampires or werewolves. Abominations, she calls them. That includes our director, Stacey."

I paused, holding the strap of my purse. "Who is a . . ."

"Werewolf. She's well aware of your last encounter. It won't be a problem." Finn strode toward the door.

I'd associated with five werewolves in my life. Two had been fellow students at college, and three had been in law enforcement. They tended toward hyperactivity and rougher sports, so they fit in well with most humans. I hadn't actually been friends with them, and from what I understood, they stuck with their own kind. My boss's boss was a werewolf. Perhaps I'd get to meet Stacey.

We exited into the hallway, turned right, and Finn stopped at the next door not four steps away. The lettering read, "Human Resources," and he opened it for me. The lights were turned off, leaving the interior in inky blackness. I rubbed the wall where I expected a switch but found none.

"You'll get used to it," Finn said as he crowded in beside me and shut the door. "Just take a step forward."

I walked through a veil into a brightly lit medical lab with two steel tables, sinks, cold storage lockers for bodies, and a steel counter that ran across the back of the room. An elaborate pewter stein rested beside a half-eaten sub sandwich. The air stunk of sharp antiseptic and maybe yeast. A dwarf with rich brown skin and purple eyes squatted on the table beside Heather Norris's body. Orange sneakers and dark green leggings showed under her white lab coat. The dwarf paused, peering at me through her round glasses.

The assistant, Udy, ignored us as he waited patiently beside the table. The bright light brought out more highlights in his brown hair. He appeared to tower over Herta by comparison.

"What?" Herta said in an annoyed tone. I found it disturbing that she stood on the same table where Heather lay, but I guessed the coroner's head would barely be above the height of the table if she stood on the floor. The sheet covered the woman's dead body up to the chest, leaving the torn flesh of the neck visible. The bulk of the skin rested to the left of her exposed spine. Her esophagus and other internal parts were gone.

Finn gestured to me. "Kristen Winters has joined the team . . ."

"And you're the oversized amoeba sent to give her the tour?" Herta placed the palm of her hand on the steel top and launched off the back of the table to the floor. "Pyre put you up to this, didn't she?"

Silently, Herta swayed from side to side as she walked around the table to face us. Her tattooed fingers dug to the side, obviously touching a realm, but I couldn't see it.

As I flinched, preparing to protect myself, Finn put

his hand on my arm. My flesh crawled with goosebumps, and a chill ran up my spine. I froze, my heart racing. Herta's rune-marked fingers whirled, and then she snapped her thumb and finger. Her hands were the length of my daughter's, yet the sound boomed and echoed in the room. The sensations across my body faded.

Udy danced forward as if she'd called a dog to heel. He carried a small tablet.

"7.36, 79, 979, 98.4," Herta rattled of a list of numbers that Udy typed in. "Have you thought about getting a cow?" she asked me.

I frowned, glanced at Finn, and pursed my lips. "Well, no."

"Considering how much dairy you consume, it might be more cost effective."

I liked cheese, but most people did. "What did you do to me?" I asked.

She dug into a realm and wiggled her fingers, causing the same racing chills and goosebumps. I saw only a shift in the air like the heat over asphalt. "Earth realm. It's odd you human witches can't control your own. Good for healing, or not. Definitely for diagnostic. Now, get out. Pyre got what she wanted." I could smell mead or beer on her breath.

"Well, what did Pyre want?" I asked.

"First, she needed you to understand who you'd be dealing with when it came to examinations that mattered. Not much question about what killed this poor woman."

Herta reached up to the top of the steel table and impossibly launched herself up to crouch on the edge. Her hair was braided into a tight tail that disappeared into the lab coat. As she stood, her purple eyes were level with mine. What I had assumed were glasses were lenses without frames, but they never wavered as she moved. They hung impossibly in place.

"Second, I can give you a relatively clean bill of health." She snapped her fingers again, making Udy — and me — wince with the force of it. "Or this navel-gazing sheep will, at least."

She appeared to indicate Udy, as he finally spoke. "Sent it."

Her eyes widened as she stared Finn down. "Get out."

Finn pulled me back into the dark veil and opened the door into the hall. I drew in a breath, standing just outside "Human Resources" and wondered if that title were some sick humor. I had never known dwarves could access the Earth realm on Earth. We had ancient grimoires about the use of the Earth realm by dwarves in the Dur-Alf realm. Could they access the Dur-Alf magic inside their own realm as Herta suggested? I had a lot of questions for Yaz when I went back to Grand Junction to visit the coven.

"Want to meet Tomas?" Finn asked with a laugh.

"Probably not." In the short minute or two with Herta, I felt abused. "Better to get it over with, though?"

"He's really not that bad. All merfolk can be a little hyper-focused, and most of his language comes from his previous time on Earth. He's one of the most efficient techs you'll meet and organized to the nines. The automatic ammo inventory is his design."

I shrugged. "Well, we've got time to waste waiting for Agent Ramirez to confirm our museum visitors. I'm hoping I have an opportunity to log in today and do some research. I'd like to feel a little more caught up."

Finn walked us to the steel door closer to the elevators. It had "Maintenance" painted on it along with an electric caution symbol. It had no handle, just a thumb pad for scanning on the door jamb. "You put your thumb here, and act as if that's what's opening the door. It's not." A click sounded, and the door popped open.

A long hall had a single dim, flickering bulb lighting the way. The door at the end had the same method of entry. Finn paused before he put his hand on the pad. "Oh, and the jacuzzi is his."

"The jacuzzi?"

"Yes. I'll give you a tour of the showers and exercise room later."

I raised my eyebrows, beginning to map out the space that Pyre's team actually occupied. The ammo room was at the end of the hall, and the elevators were close to Tomas's door. Those four rooms already took up about an eighth of one floor.

The door clicked open, and the scent of popcorn and electricity wafted out. The outer wall had a large set of windows looking over the tops of trees and buildings. To our right, two walls were filled with monitors, some angled down from the corner at the ceiling. The desk looked like a kitchen counter built out from the wall. Tomas spun his chair to face us, his right hand snapping to touch his earlobe.

Pale skinned with light, possibly green eyes, Tomas had long curly brown hair, a thin beak-like nose with tiny nostrils, gold loop earrings, an athletic figure, a handsome face, and a wedding ring. I waved and smiled sheepishly at my attractive teammate. "Hi," I said.

He wore a loose, buttoned shirt open to a hairless chest. "Kristen Winters." His tone gave no hint of emotion as he said my name in his boyish high pitch.

I had absolutely no idea what to say in response, but I flushed with a sudden wave of heat. He appeared younger than me, but when merfolk shifted to human, they created their own form, much like a dragon. Tomas might have been a couple hundred years old. Not wanting to stare like a teenager at his green-hued eyes, I scanned the monitors.

He appeared pleased at my focus, gesturing over his shoulder. "Here's your Knoxville agents' reports." Tomas ran his finger down his nose in almost a nervous tick. "They've located three of the museum visitors and confirmed their attendance. The last is already at the county courthouse where she works as a court reporter. Agent en route." Long delicate fingers pointed to a screen above and to the left with a running data search. "I'm running all unsolved museum thefts Americas-wide for the past five years. I'll boost to international when it's complete. So far, none have the same signatures."

The third monitor he indicated had a tiny picture of Jack Darcy, linked names, and a program running down a thin strip on the right side. "All known arcane and craft associates. Most are arcane with runework as their primary. One lit up with an interest in late Akkadian sigils, but they're a secondary connection." His fingers appeared full of energy, never entirely still and often touching some part of his face.

"Amazing." I would have sounded more intelligent with a pun.

"Yes." He turned and started typing.

I jumped when Finn tapped my shoulder. His hand remained, guiding me through the door. "Showers?" he asked.

I marched for the outer door, sure that despite my initial attraction, I wouldn't be crushing over a married merfolk. "Cold?"

Finn snorted and led me into the hall and pointed across to the two doors marked simply 401 and 403. "401 are archives and evidence. When the Kuru retrieve the fetter and key, they'll go there unless we find them to be talismans or imbued with any magic. In that case, they'll go to the vault." He started to continue, pointing at 403, but I interrupted.

"They're going to steal the museum's artifacts?" Oscar would have a stroke, if he hadn't already.

"Replace. Probably at the police station. No one will ever know." Since I didn't respond, he led the way to room 403. "Again, leave the hot tub alone. Tomas will know. He has never forgiven David."

The room stretched three times the width of our office. Obvious bathrooms were marked for men and women to the right on both sides of a white tiled hall. A wrapped jacuzzi sat a few feet from the men's bathroom. Two bikes, a treadmill, and a weight bench took up the back wall. Pale blue lockers formed a row beside me, and a kitchenette with a small table and chairs took the opposite side of the room to my left.

"Showers are two private stalls. Sometimes a case will keep us from getting home, and we'll get a few minutes to refresh. You'll want to keep a change of clothes here if you can." Finn pointed to the third locker. "That's yours. Tomas will encode it to you, if he hasn't already."

"I'll check in with him when I bring a change of clothes."

Finn smiled, and walked me deeper into the room. "Fridge usually smells like seafood, but I bring a lunch anyway. I keep some frozen Indian meals in there if you get hungry. Nobody else will touch them." He pointed to a door. "Towels, kitchen supplies. A cleaning crew comes in every morning around five. Leave used towels here by the door."

"This is big, for what, eight of us?"

"Three really. Me, you, and Tomas; he only uses it when no one is around. I guess Marie stores some stuff in her locker and so does David. Udy never gets a break and Herta doesn't come in here."

"Why doesn't Udy get a break?" I asked.

Finn just snapped his fingers. I wondered if he heard Herta's snap the same way I did, loud and demanding.

When we returned to the office, David sat at his desk preening in his mirror. He glanced over the metal rim as we stepped through the door. "Tour?" he asked.

Finn patted me on the shoulder and headed for his desk. "Yep."

David tilted his head with a charming smile. "You should try out the hot tub."

"I already warned her."

"Thief of joy." David frowned, then peered at his mirror and smiled. "We're dead in the water. Tomas sent the email. All visitors validated."

The information sent a cold chill down my spine. I hated when a case started to cool down. We'd tracked every lead we could think of and had missed something. Whoever had opened Tarus and let in a revenant was still out there. Without any leads, we couldn't stop them from doing it again. There were some cases when we caught a later break, and Tomas was still digging through data. The only hope I had left was that he would find an old case with similar attributes.

I looked at the cold case file but didn't open it. My most pressing objective was to learn about Iliodor and anything in the archives I thought I should know about. Dropping the folder on the top of the others in the box, I hefted them to the floor and sat at my desk.

CHAPTER
FOURTEEN

For three days after Heather's murder, I spent the morning digging into the archives, primarily learning about Iliodor. The museum investigation had stalled. I sat alone with a couple cold case files open on my desk and Finn's aftershave lingering in the office.

"I thought I said to take the day." Marie spoke behind me, and I jumped. I hadn't seen her out of her office once since Knoxville. She stepped forward and leaned a hip on the side of Finn's desk.

Finn had gone to exercise, and David left for a mysterious lunch at ten in the morning. They weren't asked to stay home.

My shoulders growing tense, I stood and motioned to the screen. "I really want to get a handle on these archives. Also, the cold cases are sort of a cleanser between sessions for me."

"You'll never finish reading the archives."

I had come to the same conclusion myself. The Iliodor wiki entries alone would take me years to read. Every report that suspected him had been linked, so I tried to focus just on the reports of verified activities, and those would take months of solid reading. "Well, there is so much I don't know."

"I didn't hire an archivist."

"Why *did* you hire me?" I'd just gotten my apartment cleaned of cardboard boxes. I should probably not stir things up.

"Because your superiors complained that you never accepted the obvious, but were right sometimes." She studied me as she spoke.

Were these complaints in my file, or had the Consociation been listening in to comments at a bar? "And, that was something you wanted?"

Marie chuckled and looked up. "I've been here for too long. I expect the same solutions to the same problems. Humans, their motives, their abilities, and technology change. Finn is not much different from me in temperament. We're always looking for a similar case that will have a similar ending. David — he has his own assets, but he's not much for getting in the mind of a criminal or cryptid."

"So, I don't know what to expect, so I look at things differently."

She shrugged. "That's part of it. What have you learned about Iliodor?"

"He's not very violent, despite being ruthless. His methods are ingenious. You've been tracking him for a very long time. He's lost anyone he loved or tried to protect. Some of them to you. I would guess he doesn't like you very much."

"Do you see him involved in this case?"

"No."

She raised an eyebrow. "Why not?"

"The fetter and key were not talismans, and neither was the ring."

The last part surprised her. "Why would you assume that?"

"I asked Tomas for a history of the ring. Delilah Madden was asked to do a psychic reading on the ring in 1987. Her psychometry is verified. She's a witch."

Marie smiled. "See?" She checked her watch and straightened. "So she didn't get anything arcane or craft off the ring."

I shook my head. "That left no motive for Iliodor. If he stole — replaced — an item at the museum with a replica, which is more his style, he wouldn't need to open Tarus. And the odds against three burglaries at once astound me. Last, he has mastered the use of Tarus, even entered the realm and escaped. He wouldn't have accidentally let a revenant loose." A smug smile fought to take over my serious expression. "We're searching for a relatively inexperienced arcane user."

"Van would have believed differently, even with this evidence."

"He was obsessed with Iliodor. Every unverified suspicion includes a report from Van. A lot are yours, too." The smile I'd been hiding, faded. I really didn't want to pack again. Marie's question and demeanor had me speaking more honestly than I might have otherwise, especially with a new boss. "Not that I'm saying you're obsessed."

"I have a healthy concern for his activities. His goals would set human society into upheaval. The ends might be a more peaceful culture, but one can't be sure. The Consociation is not willing to take that risk." She glanced at her watch. "Finn should be geared up by now. We'll meet David downstairs."

Tiberius, the cat from her office, twined around Marie's ankle. I opened my mouth to ask where the cat had come from, why Finn was gearing up, or what we were doing with David when the printer began whirring.

Her words slowly sunk in. "We have a lead?" I asked.

She just nodded toward the printer before leaning down to pet the orange cat. "Tiberius, I don't have time right now."

I took a step toward the filing cabinet where my go bag waited, then turned around for my purse to get my badge and phone. The printer continued rolling out pages, and I felt my apprehension rise. Marie strolled back into her office. The cat had disappeared.

When Finn opened the door and put the gun and ammo bags on the floor, I had the copies of the report in my hands. A cryptid described as the walking dead had killed two guards and a bank manager in Oxford, Alabama. The reports came from local FBI agents who had cordoned off the building after taking over the scene from local police. They had sequestered eight employees and customers.

"Marie?" Finn hurried behind me to the filing cabinets.

"Office."

He grunted and began pulling out our go bags. "What do we got?"

"Save it for the ride. We're driving." Marie closed her office door, strode to the bags, and grabbed David's. I didn't ask why we weren't taking the plane.

With a thud, Finn dropped mine behind me as I waited for the last page. "Heavy."

"Snacks." I knelt and stuffed the papers in the backpack. I'd added to my go bag nearly every day and hoped I'd be better prepared on this trip. From the little I'd gleaned in the archives, I wasn't going to guess this was another possessed corpse. We might be dealing with a ghoul, but if Tomas had a live video, we could see if it was feeding on the bodies.

Marie was into the hall already. "Move it!" she yelled.

Finn picked up the rifle bag and left the ammo for me to grab on the way out.

My bag was heavy, and my legs too short to keep up with Finn's long strides. Marie was already holding the elevator door. The bank didn't appear to connect to the museum case, but I wanted it to. Cold cases always nagged at me, especially when they grew frigid under my very fingers. As Finn stepped onto the elevator, I dashed down the corridor to catch up.

Outside, the day had gotten warmer, and the scent of growth mingled with exhaust. David rumbled a silver sports car into a nearby parking space as I stowed the gear in the back. He took a second to pose with his arm out the window for me. "Aston Martin DB5."

"That's nice." I shoved my go bag on top of a case of salt, grabbed a water, and stretched to pull down the hatch.

He slid out with a wave down the side. "1964. One owner. Me."

I scurried for the passenger door. Marie already had the engine running; I didn't intend to be the one keeping her waiting. She'd been casual while we talked, yet the whole time we'd had a case.

David had his door open before I did. He'd covered ten times the distance with his vampire speed.

Marie scowled at him. "Stop it. I don't need any more rumors about us, and I certainly don't enjoy explaining them to Stacey."

David flourished a hand toward the towering FBI building. "I'm already the talk of all the ladies."

"Everyone has regrets," Marie said. "You're theirs."

David buckled as she punched the SUV out of its

space, and he spoke with an amused tone. "You wound me."

Racing through the parking lot, Marie reached over her shoulder to empty air. "Files?"

"Damn." I unbuckled while the car slowed to a brisk stop, and I held to the seat before turning around to dig into my backpack. "Sorry."

We were on the highway before I'd distributed the reports. No one seemed concerned that Marie considered reading while she was driving. She grabbed a collated stack. "The first security guard, Don Peters, black male, 43, dead at 10:17 a.m., followed by Sherry Nelson, white female, 33, dead at 10:19 a.m. in the safe-deposit room. Bank manager Darren Henderson, white male, 58, reported to have been investigating the disturbance at 10:20 a.m. when a teller, Susan Kerrigan, witnessed him being torn to shreds by the walking dead."

As she read, I skimmed the report, twisting a curl.

Marie dropped a page to the center console. I refused to look out the windshield as she continued. "Susan set off the alarm and raced outside for the police. Our people had the case transferred to us. Local FBI have replaced city and county law enforcement and SWAT. Two customers fled the scene prior to the police arriving, identification pending. Finn."

"Got it, Pyre." He dialed, setting his phone to speaker. "Tomas. We need identification on the two missing customers from the bank in Oxford."

"Still don't have access to the system or live feed." Tomas swore. "We keep getting redirected to the bank manager."

David chuckled. "I could bring back that revenant."

Marie hit her papers against the steering wheel. "Tomas, is Stacey on this?"

"Yes."

We swerved, and I locked my eyes on Finn's phone, not wanting to see the road. Marie sounded more than frustrated. "Tell her she has ten minutes to get us access before I have you pop the lock." She dropped another page to the middle console. "Six bank staff and two remaining customers. We've got no witness sightings of the cryptid attempting to leave the secure area. They move fast, so I don't think the local FBI would be able to stop it, but they should see it."

David leafed through his reports. "Draugr tend to guard treasure. Maybe it's a draugr, and it senses gold or jewelry. It might decide to open a couple safe-deposit boxes."

"Well, Tarus again." I felt I stated the obvious, but no one else had mentioned it. Someone had released a cryptid from Tarus. Whatever kind it was would matter when we got there. Banks and museums both had valuables to steal. A thief with an arcane Tarus ritual had to be involved. I would assume that a witch trained in the craft would either be more skilled or careful.

Finn nodded. "I'll agree it's a breach from Tarus, but I'm not ready to connect it to the museum without some evidence. I've made that mistake before when everything is fresh in your mind."

I too had made the same assumption in more mundane cases. "Okay. How will we be able to see the video when we have access? Our phones?" If we could see the cryptid's arrival, we might have a viable lead to work from. An arcane ritual required at minimum a sigil or rune touching the realm. Banks had much better video coverage than the museum had offered.

David moved aside Marie's discarded papers, opened the center console, and slid a laptop from inside. Mounted on an arm, it moved much like a tray table in an airplane. He rotated the equipment, and it clicked into place against the dash between him and Marie. After he lifted the lid to expose the keyboard and monitor, it started booting up. We shifted a lane around a semi, and I closed my eyes, imagining Marie watching videos as we drove.

"How much longer until we get to the bank?" I asked. Hopefully I didn't sound desperate to get out of the car. No one answered.

"Access, Tomas?" Marie asked.

"It's been four and half minutes."

She snorted and veered left to avoid the back bumper of an RV with colorful bicycles clamped to the back. David rattled his breath mints. I sipped from the plastic water bottle. I'd packed an empty container, but it was tucked in my bag.

The next time Tomas spoke, he came through the laptop, so Finn hung up. "Stacey got me the access. They've got some bimbo human trying to tag along and monitor." Tomas giggled with a high-pitch. I hadn't known he would, or could find humor in anything. "He'll be a dozen steps behind. I already started downloading employee records while I kept him focused on the lobby stream."

"Keep him—" Marie started.

"From the critter feeds. Already locked him out." The monitor flickered, and both Finn and I leaned forward.

It was Finn's dreads that were scented, not some aftershave. I glanced at Marie and saw her watching the screen. Swallowing, I focused on the F7 key on the laptop.

"Here you go," said Tomas. The video opened with a fish-eye view of the safe-deposit vault with a table, three dead people, and the creature.

The cryptid, lanky with no skin covering well-developed muscles, crouched on one of the guards. Short black claws kneaded casually into the bloody mash of flesh and blue uniform that had been the man's chest. We had a side view of the vault from the back, and I could be sure the creature had no skin on its face either. Gray teeth, more carnivore than omnivore, grimaced between skinless lips. From the few drawings I'd seen, it looked like a draugr. They were described as more muscular than a ghoul and skinless. I waited for one of the others to identify it.

"Rewind," Marie said.

A black table angled at the bottom right where lockers curved under the camera. The cryptid backed up to it, circled it, then leaped off the dead manager who wore a black suit. Then the man floated up to a standing position at the door. The draugr appeared to lift the man before moving to the side as the manager backed out. The female security guard was next to rise and retreat before we came to the first guard, Don Peters. He rose with the seeming aid of the cryptid before retreating to the gate as the draugr melted into the safe-deposit boxes.

"Play. Slow." Marie didn't even glance at the road. "Stop."

The draugr sprang from the metal itself, frozen in its leap. The edges of the containers pulled slightly where it met the exposed muscles. The curving of the lens made it hard to see.

"Is there a better view?" she asked.

"No." Tomas cycled through a frame that caught the guard leaning into the gateway from the nearby hall, and a second view farther back where we could just make out his legs at the edge of the vault. That image framed the female security officer walking past a teller window toward her partner. Had he said something to alert her? We returned to the vault.

"Slow rewind."

The draugr melted into the boxes, and the man closed the gate, tapped the keypad with a card, and walked backward with a curious frown.

"He heard something—" Finn pointed to the screen "—before the draugr emerged."

I yipped as we wove between two semis without Marie even looking up. One of the truckers blew their horn. I held the back of her chair in a death grip. Finn patted my shoulder. "Looks like I'll get to use that gun."

At Marie's command, we moved the video slowly ahead as the draugr leaped through the wall, yanking the first security guard to a quick death. Even with the stream moving slow, the cryptid's speed was too fast, deftly moving out of view as the woman approached. It let her step inside before wrenching her head to an unnatural angle.

The manager ran to the open vault. A young brown-haired woman watched from the end of the hall as the draugr gutted him. It plunged a black nailed thumb into the man's eye and a finger into his ear. With a snap it threw man into the table as the teller ran off screen.

We returned to the live feed and saw it crouched as if waiting for its next challenger. That would be us. I leaned forward, looking for some markings on the boxes that might be an arcane sigil.

"A talisman in one of the safe-deposit boxes?" suggested Finn.

"Need an entity to activate it. The guard didn't get that close. Why wouldn't it have gone off during the last client to visit the room?" Marie shook her head. "Tomas. Do we have a map? What's on the other side of these boxes?"

"Steel and then the outer wall. Three feet of boxes. Two feet before air. Let me bring up the external cameras."

From a wide view of the bank and plaza, we zoomed into creme concrete walls which rose to a deep gable. There were no windows on that side. A winter-worn hedge bordered the base of the bank with tan grass leading to a sidewalk and parking lot. Black treads marked the gray bumper, but the closest car was a newer BMW parked at the far corner of the building.

A realm existed everywhere, so a cryptid could enter Earth from what appeared to be a solid wall of safe-deposit boxes. I wouldn't be able to see Tarus on a video. The problem was whoever opened it. They would have to be adjacent to the opening. Where were they?

CHAPTER
FIFTEEN

"We've got to pin the draugr as soon as we enter." Marie pulled down the offramp, barely slowing.

It had taken us an hour to get to the town in Alabama where I had expected a city. If this were a theft, I anticipated some rare and important item, and Oxford didn't seem like the place where those were common. I'd grown up in a place similar in size, and people there didn't have a lot worth stealing. Perhaps this wasn't about a theft.

Finn leaned into his door as we curved along the ramp. "Kristen, I'd suggest a shield rather than binding. Block it from exiting the vault, and I'll have you shift so I can fire."

The map of the building still sat on the laptop screen. A short, open hall ran from the lobby of the bank, beside the enclosed teller area, to the gate of the safe-deposit vault. I could block the gate opening. Moving it at the last second for Finn to fire would be the tricky part.

"Well, yes, but if it escapes around my lowered shield while you're firing, or if you miss?" Perhaps I'd create two, and leave a gap between.

"Then add another shield or bind it. Marie will be right behind us, and David can move nearly as fast as a draugr can."

Nearly as fast. David could lose more than a finger grappling with that cryptid. I peered around his chair to his lap. He'd been wearing the gloves for three days.

Marie jerked us to a stop. "I'm quick as well." Her tail had flashed by me when she skewered the corpse.

She could probably take the draugr on her own. Then again, other than silver and mercury, what did it take to kill a draugr? My grandmother's grimoire didn't usually go into those details. I knew there were spells and rituals for banishment back to Tarus. David had been able to force the revenant back into the dark realm. Was that an option with a draugr? Finn's plan implied we were going for a kill shot. I needed more time with Tomas's database. Iliodor had been a rabbit hole.

"After we kill it, then we see if there's been a robbery?" I asked. I'd dealt with safe-deposit box thefts before. Some customers claimed more loss than was actually there, and others wouldn't disclose the actual contents. I flushed with anger that we might have three dead bodies and still not be closer to the actual problem of who had released the draugr.

The light turned green, and Marie lurched the car into motion. "We'll deal with that next."

Finn offered a sympathetic smile. "They might not be connected. I believe they are, but don't focus on that at the moment. Draugrs are nasty."

We blew through a yellow light and wove through afternoon traffic. The people drove without much hurry and reacted surprised to Marie's rush. A belated horn sounded behind us.

Nine local FBI waited for us, most clustered at the front of the bank. Two black vans idled in a parking space across the lot from the entrance. The drive-thru was as large as the bank itself. More than ever, I found it hard to believe someone had anything valuable stashed there. Maybe this situation and the museum weren't connected, but I didn't believe so.

A black SUV had parked in the lane in front of the bank. Two more were parked farther down alongside vans.

We jerked to a stop and Finn unbuckled. "Grab your comms."

"Vest?" I asked.

"Locals have some for us." Finn climbed out of the Jeep.

I stepped into warmer air than we'd left in Atlanta onto tar that smelled hot. The sky was a pale blue with only threads of clouds. At least there wouldn't be any rain. A tall, glowering FBI agent separated from a cluster and approached us.

Marie gestured Finn to the hatch of the Jeep, and I went with him. She and David strode across the parking lot to engage who I assumed was the SSA assigned to this case. "Your comms. Grab enough ammo for David and Pyre." Finn unzipped the long rifle bag.

"You're not going in there until I get the full story on what the hell is going on here. The reports—" The man's tirade roared across the parking lot.

"Those reports," Marie said in a mild but firm tone, "are classified, as you've been told by your supervisor. Follow your orders to the letter, or you'll be relieved in twenty minutes and assigned to a post in Alaska investigating reports of political corruption."

"I've got a duty—" His tone hadn't eased, and he bellowed.

"Twenty minutes was an exaggeration." Marie tapped

her comms, and I hurried to shove mine in my ear, though I could hear her fine. "Tomas, SSA Hankins needs a call from his superior." She spun on her heel and strode toward us.

David paused to offer the flustered Agent Hankins a mint, and I had to smile at the man's expression.

"Tomas. Make it quick. I plan to be in gear in two minutes." She put her hand out for some of the ammo I held. "Dancing monkeys! Stacey should have had this settled by now."

David strolled toward us and stopped a couple paces away when I held up two magazines of special ammo for him. Cupping his hands he raised his eyebrows, and I guessed he wanted me to throw them to him. I frowned, placed them at the back of the Jeep, and moved to replace my own.

"Agent Hankins should be getting a call any minute." Tomas sounded pleased.

Marie didn't turn from loading her weapon, but I leaned back to see the tall man on his cell, walking away from his agents. He said something, stiffened, and peered at us. The call ended, and he appeared dazed for a moment, then turned from us and motioned to one of his people.

"Finn, Kristen, go make nice with our SSA and get us a report on the perimeter."

As I stuffed my ammo into my jacket pocket and joined Finn, an agent jogged over to one of their SUVs and began pulling out vests. We headed toward Agent Hankins. He spoke, and the group dispersed with one woman heading to intercept us.

She offered her hand to Finn. "Agent Dobbs. I'll coordinate with your team."

"Billings, Winters." Finn smiled. "What's the perimeter look like?"

"Two exits. The front and a side door." She gestured toward a corner where an agent stood. "HVAC is on the roof. We've got staff sequestered in one van and the two customers in the other. Do you want to speak with them?"

"Pyre will decide, but I believe we want to head directly inside." We accepted two vests that the male agent offered, and Finn pointed to the side door. "Double up over there and move them back about twenty-five feet."

Dobbs frowned, but nodded. "Anything else?"

"Going to sound weird, but get someone onto one of those vans to keep an eye on the roof. Just in case." Finn slipped an arm out of his jacket.

She lifted her head up to peer at the roof, then finished with a slow, unsure nod. "Okay."

We headed back toward the Jeep where David had slipped into his vest and was cinching his holster. Marie tilted her head up to catch Finn's eye. "All good?"

"Unless it comes out here."

"You're thinking of Nova Scotia. That was a jinn." Marie watched as I juggled getting my holster off and the vest on. "Move it. I want to get in and assess. Tomas, any change?"

"Draugr is still in the vault."

"What if we closed the gate?" I asked. Finn could fire through it easier than my shield.

Marie tilted her head at Finn, but asked me, "Can you bind it good enough from a distance to hold it? I can't have you get close enough to put a Dur-Alf lock on it. Do you have any idea how fast these draugr move? Or how strong?"

I didn't. However, that bothered me less than how it got to Earth in the first place. I understood Marie's priorities, but that didn't stop me from considering the obvious. What if another cryptid came through while we were fighting this one? We were missing something.

"Stick with Finn's plan. I've seen him hold a shield and fire before. Two witches make it easier." She tapped David's chest. "We'll be right behind you."

"What about whoever brought it here?" I checked my holster and it held firmly over my Kevlar.

"First things first." Marie turned and headed for the bank.

I followed last in our group. As a detective, I'd always opted for a slower pace and usually had SWAT lead. Pyre's Pups acted as both. Still, I would have needed to know where it had come from and that it was alone before I jumped in.

I drew in a deep breath and shook my head slightly. The team had experience in these circumstances, and I was new to the job. Not even a week. I frowned and focused on the draugr ahead of us.

We passed two agents who barely acknowledged us. They kept their eyes on the door. I smoothed my expression and tried to catch their eyes, but whatever had gone on with Agent Hankins and his supervisor had affected them.

"Be careful." Marie opened the lobby door for Finn and me, and we walked past posted advertising with cheerful faces.

I could sense the hurried departure from the quiet room. Papers were scattered across a black laminate counter in front of us. A chained pen dangled over its edge. A small desk sat to our right, and a glassed-in office to the left. The teller windows were in the back where a small envelope had been dropped on the floor.

Stale and sterile, the air breezed silently from vents

above the door. The room was lit by a white bowl about six feet wide and suspended from a high ceiling. The hall we were to go down stretched just long enough that I couldn't see the gate or vault from the front entrance. I dug into the moss green Dur-Alf realm and readied a shield. With my left, I scooped two fingers of the crumbling realm to prepare a binding. It hadn't worked to surprise the revenant.

David's shoes clicked on the tile floor behind me.

"It's moving," Tomas said in a quick tone, alerting us.

I threw a shield toward the hall opening, but the draugr blurred out. Gray tendons and red muscle flashed as it leaped from the edge of the hall, arcing too high to be blocked by the shield. Finn fired, and the room echoed with the gunshot.

My binding flew toward the draugr as my ears rang. The cryptid had tapped the edge of the lighting and evaded the bullet. A hole blossomed in the white ceiling. I whipped the tail end of my binding at the skinless ankle, succeeding only in tugging it off course.

A shot from behind missed the draugr, shattered the glass light, and deadened my hearing. The room darkened, and the cryptid cleared my binding with a twist. Its momentum lost, the creature dropped toward the table where the pen hung limp off the edge.

The draugr could launch toward us, and Finn would take the brunt of the attack. I'd seen how quickly the cryptid had killed.

Marie's tail rocketed past my left side, aimed toward the space over the table where the draugr would land. Finn shifted, aiming at the falling creature.

I dropped my shield by the hall and dug into Dur-Alf with both hands.

The draugr moved so fast that its arm blurred as it struck Marie's tail just behind the point. Finn fired a second time, as did David or Marie. Bullets ricocheted off the teller window, missing the cryptid as it moved impossibly fast. It used Marie's tail to fling itself to our left.

Pulse racing, I threw a shield with my right hand and a second with my left. In the spare seconds since we'd entered its domain, it had nearly reached us. When the draugr's foot touched the glass wall of the small office, it launched directly at Finn. My second shield didn't stop it, but the draugr slid across the edge. The glancing impact diverted it into the air just a pace away from the muzzle of Finn's gun. My hands trembled as my chest tightened.

It spun and twisted in the air like a fighting tomcat. Black claws raked the barrel. I could feel the screech of nail and metal even if I couldn't hear it. Finn's rifle lurched down. His third shot ricocheted off the tile below the draugr.

It had a dim glow of white to its eyes. The skinless, nearly lipless, show of teeth made it appear to grin. I thought it might crawl up Finn's gun to get to us.

My right hand's shield, carefully placed and already moving, slapped against the draugr. Its muscles, sinew, and tendons barely reacted as the stiff wall from Dur-Alf contacted the body, but it shifted the cryptid off course and stalled it.

From behind me, a bullet caught the draugr in its muscled side; the next I couldn't hear. Deafened, I witnessed the creature fling backward as a bullet entered at the cheek and opened the back of its skull. Black blood sprayed across the pale tile and shattered glass. Even as it landed, I dropped my shields and threw two bindings around the hopefully dying cryptid. My heart pounded in my throat, and I wound the spells tighter until one connected and locked.

My legs were trembling. Years ago, I'd faced down a man holding a gun to my head with more grace than I felt at the moment. Mouth open, I panted. A foul odor wafted from the motionless cryptid. Black blood oozed into a pool like spilled ink. My stomach churned from the smell, and I felt ready to retch.

I jumped when Marie patted my shoulder. "That was easy." I barely heard her, even though the comms. "Now, let's find out what brought it here."

A shiver ran through me, and I stopped breathing so I wouldn't puke like a rookie. Finn examined the barrel of his weapon. Holding a white handkerchief to his nose, David stepped up to the draugr and tapped the toe of his shoe against its skinless foot. "Perhaps one of you witches should throw an illusion over this critter. They're getting curious." He turned to peer out the entrance. We'd barely taken a couple steps into the lobby.

I couldn't hear my own words very well. "I'm not very good with illusions. Best I could do is a shadow."

Finn motioned for me to attempt it.

Digging both hands into Mer, I scooped out a gelatinous wad of blue-green and pushed it toward the draugr. The pleasant color faded as it hit flesh and rolled across in a mottled fog of gray and black.

David raised his eyebrows at me. "You do suck. I thought with all that quick magic that you could make a gorilla or something out of it."

I turned toward the vent to take a breath, but the reek permeated the room. We had to find out how it got in the bank, and that meant working in the vault with three dead bodies. Shaky, I just wanted some water and fresh air. That would have to wait.

"How long will it hold?" Marie gestured toward the fog covering the draugr.

"Fifteen minutes or so." I had never practiced with it much. "We should check the vault."

Marie frowned. "Agreed."

CHAPTER
SIXTEEN

A single bloody, misshapen footprint painted the hall to my right. I stood at the gate to the vault, sweating from nerves and exertion. Pulling that much from the realms in one short minute always had a cost. My ears still rang, but I could hear.

Finn stood ahead of me with Marie at the edge of the dark pool surrounding the three bodies. The first guard's chest had been shredded beyond definition of shirt, flesh, or bone. His viscera stunk like a sewer.

David ran his hand over the wall of safe-deposit boxes, pulling up sparkling gray wisps of the Tarus realm in a display I'd never seen before. "Oh yeah. It's all over these. Not one little spot, but this whole central area."

My eyes widened and I glanced at Finn, though he didn't appear surprised. I could see realms when I touched them, or a witch near me did, and when I touched a vampire, werewolf, and evidently a dragon-shifter. I had never witnessed a realm's reaction to anyone other than another witch. No witch had, that I knew of. Now I saw David interacting with a remnant of

Tarus. Someone like my daughter might be that sensitive to see a leftover trace on a physical object, but I doubted it.

Marie studied the bodies, peeking around the central table to see the floor at David's feet. His shoes had left pale imprints in the dark blood where thickening liquid had been pushed aside. "Any other evidence?"

David peered at his feet. The pool of blood from the three bodies left only a foot of exposed tile in the back by the lockers. "Nope. What a waste."

I frowned when I realized he indicated the blood, not the people or lack of evidence. If we were stymied again, then the person responsible for Heather's death and the bodies on the floor might have escaped to continue releasing the inhabitants of the Tarus realm. My lips tightened as I remembered the haunting expression on Heather's daughter's face. What family did the people on the floor have?

I drilled into the solution, not the consequence. "Could they have opened Tarus in an adjoining room or outside, and the draugr came out here?"

Marie turned and focused on me. "We're talking three feet of metal boxes on all sides except the front. I could see a revenant traveling through that, but not a draugr. Still, we should check the adjacent walls, including outside." She stopped as the front doors of the bank opened.

The rattle of metal and wheels spoke of Udy and Herta arriving. Marie frowned and turned back to the bodies. I stepped away from the gate, making room.

Udy pulled a gurney behind a squat, mustached man in a stained lab coat. The illusion of Herta had a badge pinned to his lower stomach in an awkward placement. Thinning wisps of hair contrasted a thick mustache. A long, impossible glob of snot hung out the left nostril, clung to hairs on the upper lip, and swung almost down to the illusion's chin.

I couldn't help but wipe my own face. This had to be payback on Udy's part for Herta's sharp personality.

"Air-wasting piles. You're tracking the whole place up without booties." The illusion managed a scowl, though both eyes focused toward the nose when it did so. I could recognize Herta's voice, and it didn't blend well with what Udy had created.

I almost mentioned that the draugr had left the footprints in the hall, but Herta might have meant David. I sidled along the wall of the corridor, letting the coroner come through while I aimed for the lobby; Finn followed suit. Marie stepped back but remained intent on the wall of metal drawers.

Herta threw a hand out when David circled the bodies and blood, aiming for the front of the vault as if to head down the hall. "No, put on the booties." She had a strange pronunciation of the last word, elongating the vowels.

"They don't go with my suit."

Marie finally relinquished the vault and turned to step past Herta. "We're going to have to be careful with trace on these." She gestured to the bodies.

Udy stepped around the gurney and offered two plastic booties to David. Finn and I stopped where the hall met the lobby, waiting for Marie. The malodor from the blending of dead draugr and viscera made me want to gag.

David marred his usually handsome face and scowled at the plastic. He caught me watching him, so when he lifted his blood covered sole, he drew a finger through it instead of putting the bootie over it. Locking eyes with me, he tasted the blood. "Mmm. A little stale."

"Stow it." Marie walked toward me. "Kristen, take

David to the adjacent walls and have him test for any sign of Tarus as you suggested. I don't know what it means if we find anything. This doesn't make sense. Finn and I will start the interviews. Staff first."

"Okay." I preferred working with Finn, but David would have a better sense of the Tarus realm.

She stopped and studied me. "Keep at it. Whatever is churning inside there might be the answer."

I flushed, assuming she complimented me. "We'll likely need access to the teller's room." I pointed to the glass and the exit on the corner opposite us beside the drive-thru windows.

"Do the outer perimeter first, then get with that Agent Dobbs. She can get a key or card from one of the tellers."

There was an audible click and buzz from the teller room. Tomas spoke over the comms. "I can get you in. Just let me know when you're ready. It auto locks."

Herta berated Udy from the back room as David joined us.

I looked forward to fresh air. "Let's do the outer wall first."

Marie prodded Finn toward the front exit. "You're with Kristen, David. Comms on."

David smiled at me. "Our first date." He rattled his mints.

"Over my dead body." I smiled and then pointed at his booties. "I need a picture."

His smile drooped. "Try it and you *will* be a dead body. This is mortifying."

Glass crunched under our feet as we passed my shadow covering the draugr. I half expected it to burst forth, but its brains trailed a good distance from the pool of black blood.

Outside, the fresh air smelled like growing grass, and I

couldn't breathe enough of it. It felt like I inhaled the blue sky.

FBI peered at us from their positions in the road. Agent Dobbs nodded to us, though her supervisor was nowhere to be seen. I hoped he hadn't been transferred to Alaska. Somehow, I believed Marie could do that.

I glanced behind me to the lobby. The windows were dark and slightly reflective. The agents might have seen motion or heard shots, but they wouldn't have had a clear view of the draugr.

David squinted and looked uncomfortable in the bright sunlight, but he'd lathered up with his strange concoction when we'd neared Oxford. We walked under the drive-thru to circle the building. An agent patrolling around the corner seemed surprised to see us. He glanced at David's booties.

A few feet of tan grass with green shoots grew from the base of the bank to the sidewalk. David stopped there and removed the plastic to wipe his soles. "I am not walking in public with these." He held them out for me to take.

I reached and nearly took them. He wanted me to walk around with them in my hands like the stupid newbie. "No." I snorted and paced down the sidewalk.

Pale stuccoed walls needed the dust and perhaps pollen washed off them. The extended eaves sheltered the camera at the far corner of the building. Shrubs barely held their green against the base.

Over the comms, a van door opened, and Marie introduced herself. Midway, she turned off her comms.

The outer wall of the building looked longer than I expected. "Tomas, we're on the back side of the building. Can you estimate the location of the back of the vault?"

He swore as if I had asked a stupid question. "You're

eighteen inches from the corner of the room, and over nine feet from the center."

I took four steps and pointed at the cement wall. "This is the center?" I asked. The bushes at the base were dry and smelled musky.

"Close enough."

David stood so close to me that I jumped when I turned to look at him. Sometimes he moved noisily, and other times he'd be by my side without a hint of movement.

I swallowed and gestured. "Do you want to check here?"

He'd been smiling at my flinch, but now he grinned, and handed me the nasty booties. This time I took them as I stepped back.

David's search brought tendrils of the Tarus realm off the surface. "That's odd," he said.

It still boggled my mind that I could see it, but he referred to the fact that the effect happened inside and out. "Strange," I agreed.

I studied the side of the building, the plants, the sidewalk, and eventually the parking lot. There were few cars on this side. Two black smudges on the concrete curb looked as if they'd been made by tires. "Tomas, can I get a video playback on my phone? I need the lot before the draugr appeared until after it emerges in the vault."

"Sending you a link now via email." Tomas's high-pitched voice held no emotion, not even his usual annoyance.

I pulled out my phone, and David moved to my shoulder, a bit too close for my comfort. He kept his back to the sun. The link opened a video that I stopped immediately. We had a wide view, and smack in the middle was a short black trailer hitched to a white Ford; they both appeared rather new. The back doors of the trailer were open, covering most of the sidewalk we stood on now.

"Tomas, is that vehicle lined up with the vault?"

He response sounded pleased. "Yes. It belongs to the same company, Lamb's Lion, Inc., who left the trailer in Knoxville. I'm pinging Pyre."

I saw no identifying marks. "How do you know it's theirs?"

Tomas swore. "I'm not an idiot."

David shrugged when I glanced over. I let the video continue. The doors remained open for a while, then a short, muscular man closed them with a casual move.

Marie spoke through her comms. "What is it, Tomas?" Her tone was polite, but short.

I paused the video as the man locked the back of his trailer. My choice would have been to ask Tomas a few more questions before we bothered her.

"I've sent you the link requested by Winters. There's a connection to the Knoxville case that you'll want to review."

"Thank you. Kristen, where are you?"

I took a deep breath. "At the back of the building. David found traces back here, so I asked for the video playback of the back lot for before the draugr arrived."

"Wait. I'll be right there. C'mon."

I assumed the last comment was for Finn, so I straightened myself and shook off my concerns. Continuing the video, I watched the man as he stood up after locking his trailer. He wore jeans and a tight white T-shirt. His hair was closely cropped, and his face clean-shaven. Yellow tinted glasses hid his eyes.

He walked casually out of sight on the far side of the trailer, then reappeared with no apparent hurry to open the driver's door of the Ford. Only one concerned glance back at the building confirmed my suspicions. A flash of fear washed over his expression before he climbed in and drove away.

The front of the truck turned toward the camera, and there was no plate visible. "Tomas, how do you know the truck belongs to the Lamb company?"

"Trust me. I know. There are more than just the damned bank cameras." His tone admonished, and I cringed.

"Okay. Sorry."

Marie turned the corner, watching her phone as she walked. "Don't let Tomas bully you. So, the same company that left the trailer in Knoxville. Tomas, I want an address."

"Sent it to your email. Owner Fitz Dunn. Facial recognition confirmed with video."

Marie stopped, still not looking up, and I belatedly followed David as he approached her. "Damn good, Kristen," she said.

I shuffled and flushed, unsure of her compliment and not wanting to appear cocky. "Thank you. I still don't know what he's doing."

David passed her as if heading to the front of the bank. Finn gave me a supportive smile and nod. I slowed a few steps away from them, soaking up a moment of Finn's recognition. I'd helped some since joining the team and fumbled my magic a couple times, but this lead made me reassess my concerns and consider that I did have something to add.

She turned and followed David. "Move it."

Finn spun to join their group and I was left trailing them and double-stepping to catch up. We had a chance to stop Fitz Dunn before he got someone else killed.

CHAPTER
SEVENTEEN

As we reached the front parking lot, Udy climbed inside a white step van and dragged a body bag into it from the gurney. He gave a slow wave when he spotted us. My stomach growled, and I smiled thinking about the snacks in my go bag. We'd driven to the bank close to lunchtime, and the sun had lowered during our engagement with the draugr and our investigation. I had no idea where we were headed in Georgia, but I could be sure we weren't stopping to eat.

Marie marched for the jeep like a freight train. David used long strides to keep a pace ahead. Finn's legs easily ate up the distance, and I nearly jogged. She'd be in no mood for dawdling.

"Where the hell are you going?" Agent Hankins hopped out of a black SUV and stomped toward us.

Marie didn't slow. "Finn. When will that foyer be clear?"

I almost plowed into him as he paused to balance the long rifle while he dug for his phone. Offering my hand, I took the weapon. Watching Udy and Hankins, I moved to the back hatch of the Jeep.

Agent Hankins's face had shaded red with anger. "You're not dumping this on me." Still a few parking spots away from us, he had to bellow, drawing the attention of his agents.

"No," Marie said as she reached the driver's door, "we're not. You'll make sure we've got full reports on all the witnesses before you release them."

"Kuru is already here." Finn spoke quietly, but it came through the comms.

Tucking the weapon among our bags, I peered over each shoulder before I found the red and green taco truck parked deeper in the plaza. David's door closed, then Marie's. I propped my go bag behind my seat so it would be easier to reach.

"You can't tell me they're clear to go inside." Agent Hankins swore as he passed Udy and found Marie already starting the Jeep. "Are you—" He stopped as Marie's window rolled down.

I closed the hatch and slid around the side where he faced Marie. She casually dropped an elbow out her window, glanced at me in the side mirror, and smiled at him. "Communications will call when they can bring in crime scene cleaners."

Tomas swore.

I offered a weak smile as I opened my door, not wanting to bump Agent Hankins. He ignored me, saving his glare for Marie.

Marie's tone bristled. "Move back. We need to leave. The coroner will give communications the all clear."

Tomas sighed. "I'll contact Udy."

I squeezed in, though Agent Hankins didn't budge. Finn had pulled both our go bags up to the front, and I beamed at him. The car smelled like David's mints. I eased the door shut, hoping it had closed all the way. The Jeep shifted as Marie put it in reverse. I fumbled for my seatbelt.

"All of this will be in my report. I'll be submitting a personal complaint of your behavior." His voice rose as she began rolling up her window.

Marie eased the Jeep back. "Pyre with a 'Y.' It's your career." The car dash dinged. "Close your door, Kristen."

I grimaced before opening the door quickly and slamming it shut. Agent Hankins glared as we left him. How often did local enforcement and the FBI have this issue? All witches whispered about the Consociation running governments like puppets, but we really didn't know the details. History had proved that mundanes obsessed over cryptids and witches.

"Tomas. ETA?" Marie punched the gas as she drove forward.

"An hour to Atlanta, maybe more. It'll be heavy traffic. Hour and a half east to Athens. I've emailed you the coordinates to his office."

"Night storms. No way around it. Do you have his phone signal?" Marie wove through the parking lot and didn't stop as we launched onto the main road.

I slunk deep into my seat and focused on silently unzipping my backpack.

"He's in Athens. Likely at his office. Not a lot of cell towers for the area." Tomas sounded annoyed.

"Tomas, dig up everything you've got on Fitz Dunn." Marie gestured toward the console for David to ready the laptop.

"That's what I'm doing." He swore and mumbled.

I slid a lemon-flavored protein bar out and grimaced as it crinkled. We had a long ride ahead, and I hoped we'd stop for gas so I could pee.

Finn handed me a warm water. "Good catch on the trailer. You did good in there today."

"Good?" I used my question to mask the tearing of the package. "Well, I fumbled most of the shields."

He shook his head, dreads swinging. "Not the ones that mattered. Gave me a clean shot. Draugr are fast. I should have known that it would expand its territory. Usually they nest near the treasure for a while, then scout out a zone of protection. We found one in east Alberta that had been guarding twenty gold coins in a cabin for twelve years. The owner had botched the summoning, and no one knew until the property was selling and a building inspector disappeared."

I slid the bar out of the open wrapper. "Were you on the case?"

"I was. Me, Pyre, Van, and a werewolf named Bethany. She was a terror."

David leaned off his seat, speaking without turning around. "But you were thrilled when you found out I'd be replacing her."

Finn rolled his eyes. "Beyond words."

I chewed quickly. The protein bar tasted less lemon and more something else — without much flavor. "Bethany, did David replace her because she died?" Van's death had me wondering about the life expectancy of Pyre's Pups.

"No. She's living with her son and grandkids in Miami."

I stuffed the wrapper in my pack. "How did you stop the draugr in Alberta?"

"Bethany shifted. She and Pyre pinned the draugr. Me and Van both shot it." Finn scratched an eyebrow and frowned. "Gary wanted me to retire about that time. I almost did. However, Bethany left. It's the only thing me and Gary really argue about." He tapped on the cap of his water bottle with one finger. "I'm going to be fifty this year."

"God that's old," David said with an exaggerated tone.

"Bethany was fifty when she retired from Pyre's Pups. She runs a security consulting firm." Finn sounded a little remorseful.

I hadn't meant to dig into any bad memories for Finn. Changing topics was easy since I'd been mulling on something that no coven had ever prepared me for. "Well, Herta used Earth realm magic; is that common for people from other realms?"

Tomas intercepted my question. I'd forgotten he was on the comms. "Of course. Amazing healing magic — which is surprising once one actually meets humans."

Finn had turned toward the window, appearing to be deep in thought with his thumb on his chin and two fingers on his lips. I decided to let the conversation drop. Tomas had work to do, and my questions could wait until we weren't neck deep in a pursuit.

I gazed at my backpack. Protein bars do not fill you up as much as they should. In the midst of opening my second bar, the laptop between Marie and David blinked with a new screen.

A series of pictures filled the monitor. All of them were of a man close to my age, in his thirties, with well-trimmed brown hair and no other identifying marks. When he smiled, he appeared engaging and friendly. Otherwise, he was mildly attractive and likely forgettable. Tomas reported briskly and shared screens as he spoke. "Fitz Dunn is a fake identity and only active for seven years. No facial recognition to any other identity. No social media except for a couple inactive accounts supporting his business. Lamb's Lion, Inc. became active five years ago when it commenced. The last two years it has had little recorded income and primarily maintenance expenditures with cash infusions into the account. The Dunn identity has no criminal record. One parking ticket two months ago."

"Were there any robberies reported in the vicinity at that time?" I asked.

Marie nodded.

We were silent for a moment before Tomas swore. "Yes. Jewelry from the store his trailer was ticketed at."

Somehow, Fitz Dunn, or whoever he was, used the Tarus realm to commit his robberies.

Marie spoke crisply. "Tomas. Please scan the list of customers who own safe-deposit boxes on the outer wall. Make me a list of any who pop up who might have jewelry above an average value. We'll be having them check their boxes with Agent Hankins or Dobbs."

We had plenty of motive, a means that eluded my understanding, and a suspect who had been at multiple locations. If we caught him, we might learn how he managed the robberies.

David rattled his mints. "I've got dibs on an artifact. Maybe a new one we haven't identified."

Marie tilted her head. She was threading through heavy traffic. "Finn?"

He sighed and straightened. "I'm with Kristen's original assumptions. Unintentional consequences of an arcane ritual. One we've never heard of."

She glanced at the mirror, but didn't ask me. "I'm going to need gas before we get there. Hold it for a while longer. I'll stop soon."

Over an hour later, after we had crawled through Atlanta, Marie stopped on the east side of the city to let us use the restrooms.

The drive to Athens she took at a breathtaking speed,

and I kept my eyes off the road, focusing on nibbling at some cheese and crackers I'd picked up at the gas station. The sun dropped lower behind us and lit the headrest in front of me with gold.

Tomas had left the screen on a map of Athens overlaid with a green circle showing Fitz's mobile location. He could have been anywhere, but a red marker showed his office and our projected arrival time. Tomas injected no emotion or opinion into his comment when he came back onto the comms. "You're about an hour out. You haven't called for local response."

"Too dangerous," Marie said. "If his magic helps him elude discovery, then a cordon of FBI or SWAT would just trigger his magic. I'd rather be there to contain any unintentional consequences."

As we arrived at the edge of the city, thick woods, scattered residences, and businesses cropped up on the outskirts of the highway. A couple stoplights frustrated Marie. Once we passed a major exchange and crossed another highway, the forests disappeared, and businesses crowded our busy road. The city proper grew slowly around us until older brick buildings dominated the sides of the streets.

The laptop showed a map of the first floor of the office building with the Lamb's Lion office outlined. A hall ran from a front door to multiple offices. I could easily make out a bar at the front of the building.

With no parking on our side of the street, Marie swore and swerved in a U-turn to pull into an angled spot in front of an old seven-story building where our suspect had an office. The few cars outside were neither trucks nor trailers. There was a tight parking garage across the street, but I didn't imagine even a short trailer would be fun to navigate through that. A police substation occupied the first floor of the garage.

I peered down the street. "Well, no trailer."

"Mm-hmm." Marie shoved the Jeep into park and turned off the engine.

Frowning, I unbuckled my belt. It was obvious to everyone that no black trailer was on the street. My pulse rose, partially embarrassed and more so because we were about to confront someone who could and had drawn creatures from the Tarus realm.

Finn stepped out of the Jeep. "Pyre, rifle?"

Two women were walking down the sidewalk watching us. A delivery man hurried from the other direction with a small box under his arm. Cars passed behind us, adding the heavy scent of exhaust to otherwise fresh air. Eyes lingered on us in our FBI vests and wearing holsters.

"Afraid so," she said.

Old iron railings and columns, dark modern windows, and faded, white brick walls made up the building ahead of us. The center doors led inside to the hall where Fitz Dunn's office waited. Marie and David quickly led the way, leaving me and Finn to scramble. Unfortunately, the two women stopped and watched us from a few yards away. If something nasty came out of the building, we'd have a hard time containing it.

I trailed last in our group into an empty hallway where Marie and David already inspected an old wooden door with a frosted glass window. Fitz's company logo and name were painted in silver and gold. Marie stood a pace back. Of course David trailed his hands on the door frame. No wisps of Tarus emanated from the frame as it had at the bank. He'd stopped wearing his gloves, and his new finger was pinker than his nearly white skin. Finn was already tugging on Dur-Alf, so I tested Mer, though few wards used that realm.

"Pyre, I don't see anything," Finn said.

"Open it."

If Fitz Dunn wasn't inside, we'd surely be setting off an alarm. As Finn pulled at the Mer realm, I dipped my fingers into the dry, crumbling Dur-Alf and threw a shield between him and the door. After dealing with Blake, rather Jack, I didn't trust any of these magic users. In all my years on the force, I had to adjust to the different threats to expect. The stream from Mer swam around my shield and flowed over the old lock, seeping into the doorjamb.

I heard the click, and David immediately slipped around my shield, opened the door wide, and led the way. An alarm panel to the left beeped off a countdown. My pulse rose as Marie stepped in next. Fitz wasn't here.

The front office had a small desk with a computer monitor barely two steps from the front door. Cardboard boxes piled around the room. Three mannequins clustered in a back corner, nearly hidden. Shelves near the ceiling held smaller boxes. Stale dust drifted from our steps in the musty room. Marie swore under her breath, but I could hear over the comms.

Finn tugged frantically at Dur-Alf as David opened another door leading to more cluttered storage in a room dimly lit by a small window. I stepped onto the wood floor, hand on my holster, though I didn't expect anyone.

Tomas swore. "He's turned off his cell."

Marie stopped at the door to the room where David searched. "He doesn't sleep here. Upstairs? Tomas, does he have rentals or own any other properties?"

"Nope. Vehicles. Six trailers and three trucks. Paid them off in the past four months."

I spotted the first camera, small and innocuous, on a

shelf between two boxes. "Surveillance." I gestured toward it, then a second and third all in the front room.

"I'm hitting the building's Wi-Fi now." Tomas swore as the alarm rang behind us, drowning out the comms.

My pulse raced in response to the siren. Finn dragged fingers into Dur-Alf and sent a wad toward a white disc resting on a pile of boxes. He crushed the unit in a spray of sparks, and the noise stopped.

"Pyre, I don't have an attempted video feed from that office," Tomas said. He sounded loud after the moment of silence. "Plenty of others in offices and apartments. I'd have to be on site to find what he's using and track it."

"You're an hour out. Move it. We need to find out where he's holed up." She smacked the vest she wore. "He knows we're onto him."

"Hour and a half," Tomas said before cursing.

I'd finally contributed a solid lead to the team, and he hadn't been here. We had a face and a fake name. If we didn't find Fitz Dunn, he'd remake his identity and start again with the ring from the museum and whatever he'd gotten from the bank. We were dealing with a simple thief, probably a mundane with a ritual, who used Tarus recklessly. We were probably as close as we'd been in the entire case.

"Tomas," I asked, "are there any traffic cams we can search for his trailer, or trailers?"

Marie nodded. "Also, contact local enforcement to ignore the alarm. We're locking the door, and it's off limits. FBI business."

CHAPTER
EIGHTEEN

"I've got the door." I stepped into the hall and nodded to an older man who stood outside one of the businesses, watching us.

Finn joined me. Marie darted straight for the onlooker. "Agent Pyre with the FBI." She pulled out her badge. "We're looking for the tenant Fitz Dunn; do you know him?"

He peered at us warily and shook his head. "Seen someone go in there, time or two. That's it."

"Understood. The building manager, or leasing office, are they in the building?"

The lease would likely have a residence marked on it, even though it might be false. Perhaps Fitz didn't consider it when he initially signed for the office.

"Kelly's Realty. They got a sign up front." He turned, reaching for his door.

"Thank you, Sir. Do you know any of the other tenants who had contact or a relationship with Fitz Dunn?"

He opened his door. "Nope."

Marie nudged her chin toward the exit. "Finn, let's put

that in the Jeep." I assumed she meant the rifle. "David, call the realty people and get an address for Fitz. Tomas is busy."

David bowed and strode for the door. "On it, Pyre." In two steps, he beat Finn.

The hallway empty, I pulled a handful of crumbling Dur-Alf realm and spread a lock on the door jamb, but just at the handle. Tomas would need to break in if I weren't available. A Dur-Alf lock was keyed to the person who placed it.

I turned to find Marie studying me. "Thoughts?" she asked.

Following her lead, we headed for the door. "Well, he's got to store his trailers somewhere. We know he's in Athens, or was until a couple minutes ago. It would make sense that he came from the bank job to store equipment and stash whatever he stole. Just not here." I gestured to the office door.

Tomas audibly closed a door on the comms. "The city cams are crap. I've got a program running on the few available in case he has driven by one of the schools."

The exhaust outside seemed to have grown thicker. David's comms off, he talked on the phone, smiling at the woman passing him. Finn had the back hatch of the Jeep open.

Marie stopped on the sidewalk and faced me. "So, we drive around and check every lot in the vicinity? It'll be dark in a short bit."

"Well, I guess." I glanced down the street. Shadows hung off the buildings into the road. The first floor of Fitz's building was already dark. An old Jack Daniel's sign clung to the bar's window. I tilted my head and touched my curls. "Maybe Fitz likes a drink on occasion. Let me try something."

Removing my holster, I headed for the Jeep and piled holster, badge, and Kevlar into my seat. Without my suit jacket, I could have been any professional. I patted my curls to make sure they covered my comms, grabbed my purse, and headed back to Marie. "Give me two minutes."

David pocketed his phone and came up with mints. "I've got an address. Of course."

"Two minutes. Move it," Marie said to me, then she and David gave the address to a cursing Tomas as I headed for the bar door.

I dabbed on fresh lipstick as I walked. I tried for my best relaxed walk as I passed the tinted window, aiming for professional, but open to conversation. The last time I'd been to a bar, it had been with three other detectives and the room had been full of cops. In this scenario, I needed to act like I was on a friendly date; I hadn't been on one of those in a long while.

The late afternoon sunshine left the room a dark pit when I stepped inside. The bartender nodded from the back where a large u-shaped bar surrounded her. On the right side, a young man, a barback by his towels, stood with an elbow on the polished counter a few seats down from a morose older man staring at his glass. Two women sat engrossed in a conversation to the left of me. Two of the tables by the windows on each side of the door were taken up with pairs of drinkers.

The room stunk of stale beer with a note of something fruity and alcoholic. I caught the eye of the barback and smiled as I strode straight for the bartender. She had that pleasant but not smiling face that many of her trade mastered. The disheveled barback grinned easily, straightening and wiping his hands.

"A quick beer while I wait." I motioned to her tap, naming what seemed a local beer. "Thanks." Watching them both as I dug in my purse, I targeted the barback. I paid and sipped at my beer, wandering over to gaze at a picture on the wall, then glanced at the door as if expecting someone.

"Do not tell me someone stood you up." The barback had no real chin.

I smiled. "I left him a message. I'm looking for Fitz; has he been in tonight?"

His smile faded, but didn't disappear. "Not yet. Did you try his office?"

Taking another sip, I shrugged. "Didn't answer the door. He's not responding to his text. No big deal. Just thought I'd say hi while I was in town."

The barback regrouped. "I'm Sam. I work the days." A weak way to tell me he was off this evening. "Where are you from?"

His name annoyed me, but no one could compete with Sam Winchester from Supernatural. "Glenwood Springs, Colorado. I'm in Georgia for a bit. I was hoping to hang for a while, but if Fitz is out, I'll just head off and wait until he texts."

"He's probably over at his storage unit. He'll be here." His chin disappeared even more as his lower lip rose.

Tomas grumbled. "Checking closest now."

As I just returned to sipping my beer, Sam forced his smile. "What's your name?"

"Athens storage on Wilkerson." The comms crackled as Tomas spoke. "Eight minutes from your location."

"The storage over on Wilkerson?" I asked.

"Yeah, that's the one." He nodded enthusiastically, happy to help.

I handed him my beer. "I'll be back." Strolling for the door, I tried to ignore the sound of the Jeep starting in my comms. Clear of the front window, I ran before Marie left me behind.

David grinned ear to ear from his front seat. "Aren't you the little minx. Should have got his number."

I flushed and Finn just shook his dreads with a grin.

"Stow it, David." Marie sounded impatient as I hurried into my seat.

As soon as I closed my door, she punched it into reverse. Someone blew their horn, but we managed to avoid getting hit as she tore through the shaded city. We swerved onto a local road with residential apartments before I got my seatbelt fastened.

"You're going to need this." Finn lifted my vest.

"That and a gun might be good." I'd started to sweat when we were breaking into Fitz's office, but running had me hot. As Marie raced down curving streets, I stowed my purse, and working around my seatbelt, managed to get all my gear back on.

The city turned into a residential neighborhood with two- and three-story buildings, then dropped to rural outskirts in a blink of an eye. Automotive garages and yards sprang up, and we flashed past a gas station as Marie passed on a double line.

I didn't dare lift my head again until Finn spoke. "Up there, on the left." He gestured to the side of the street, and I peered out my window.

Rows of low gray buildings had almost dull red bay doors. Fences with barbed wire lined the perimeter toward the street, but I could see between the six buildings as Marie raced past. Far in the back of the middle buildings, a black trailer was pulled close to an open bay door. We'd tracked down Fitz.

"There," David and I spoke at the same time.

At the end of the buildings, the entrance from the road

turned sharply, and Marie slowed to a turn without squealing the tires; the motion had me nearly butting heads with the back of her seat. One part of the drive led up a low hill to more buildings and some U-Hauls. To our immediate left was the locked gate to the rows of storage bays and the code box to get in.

We tugged to a stop, Marie slammed the Jeep into park, and I stared at heavy fence easily as high as me topped with nasty looking barbed wire. As doors opened, I fumbled for my seatbelt.

"Finn?" Marie asked as she leaped out.

"Got it, Pyre."

By the time I stepped onto the asphalt, Finn had rounded the back of the Jeep, and two blue-green trails of the Mer realm were shooting for the gate. One aimed at the end where the rolling section rested at a static pole, and the other into the motor mechanism. I was impressed when the entire gate hitched an inch off the track and clicked. It scraped back enough to let Marie through. I'd have to ask Finn later what he'd done.

"Kristen, with me." Marie motioned Finn and David down the front of the buildings, and I chased behind her as she angled for the back.

The shadows were deep and left only the tops of the low buildings lit. Cool, fresh air made the Kevlar a little more bearable as I ran.

When we turned the corner and raced down the back, I was relieved to see the nose of a white truck beyond the end of the middle building. We'd know if Fitz started to leave. Marie kept a pace or two ahead, partially because she moved faster than me.

"No sign of our suspect," Finn said over the comms. "Trailer doors are open."

They would have reached their end of the row first and

were moving up the drive between the two buildings. Marie barely slowed as she reached the corner. I could smell the hot engine of Fitz's truck, but it wasn't idling. He might know we were searching for him, but he hadn't expected us to find him here.

Marie slowed as we took the corner, and we stalked between his truck and a closed bay door. David and Finn had crept toward us and were about a bay away from Fitz's open storage unit. Finn had his weapon out, but I kept the Dur-Alf realm in mind. I wanted to capture Fitz, not put a slug with mercury into him. Just in case of wards, I tugged on Dur-Alf, but nothing showed.

Marie whispered into her comms. "One."

Inside, a grid wall rested on the ground near the entrance by Finn.

"Two."

What sounded like small metal parts clattered.

"Three."

We broke around the corner of the opening, and I had to take an extra step to clear myself around Marie. David just strolled in.

The bay was deep, a good twenty feet to the back wall. Displays and parts lined the right side, but Fitz rose from a line of cardboard boxes on the left straight ahead of my position. Even as he locked eyes with me, he dropped a black satchel and ran for the back corner. My fingers dug through dry Dur-Alf to create a binding, and I whipped it down the bay.

My dark green stream splashed futilely off the back of his hoodie and faded into mist. Fitz placed the fingers of his right hand on an Akkadian sigil already detailed on the metal wall.

David flashed through the bay in a strolling blur of his black suit and white cuffs. Marie's golden tail dove quickly over the few boxes and against the wall like an arrow. I feared that she'd skewer the man.

Fitz's sigil sparkled, fading from the wall. Where his hand touched, the realm of Tarus billowed around him, and the metal wall moved. Amazed, I watched with an intense, morbid curiosity. I had never heard of anything like this. There was no sound, but the ribbed steel stretched away from us as if fashioned from cloth.

Marie swore as her tail touched Tarus and she whipped it back. "Night storms."

David froze in place, warily eying the gray mist. He likely didn't notice the back wall puckering as he spoke. "This is new." Finally, he took a step back.

Finn slid into position in the bay with his gun ready; he pointed to the side with David in his way. I didn't see a target. I drew and raised my weapon, unsure in that first moment what I would do. Then I ignored the trippy metal wall and rolling cloud of Tarus to aim where I had seen the sigil.

My shot and recoil snapped me back into focus. The wall returned as if it had never moved. Gratefully, the silver, mercury, or other elements in the bullet had been enough to break the ritual.

Fitz flopped backward, staggering then dropping to his rump. It didn't appear that I'd hit him.

A dread poured through me as the Tarus realm shivered and phased away. I staggered and nearly dropped my weapon. Unreasonable panic grew and reached cold fingers around my heart and squeezed.

David tilted forward as a new cloud formed. "A demon," he called out. Pitch as night, it barely had shape.

Stricken with fear and trembling, I lowered my gun before I did shoot someone by mistake.

The demon's head formed from a cloud of chaos.

Dozens of white eyes rolled across the surface of an almost human skull. It breathed terror into me. I'd heard stories, but my horror grew with every thudding beat of my heart. It fed me dismay and feasted on my emotion.

An arm formed with a single finger and perhaps a thumb. It picked up Fitz and threw our suspect across the bay, as if with disdain. A second appendage grew and dove a too long finger into David's chest.

Marie fired, but her bullet appeared to have no effect, or she'd missed.

The demon's head tilted.

"No!" I screamed. Some odd piece of courage shot my hand in the dust of the Dur-Alf realm. The binding that I threw curved along the demon, finding an edge to hold onto.

Even as the terror raced at me, I curved my grip tighter trying to get the tip of the binding to touch itself around the demon. If I could succeed, it would be bound. Already I pulled at Dur-Alf with my left hand readying another binding.

Marie fired a second shot.

Six appendages had sprouted out of the cloud by this time. The nightmare raced toward us. Toward me. Grasping pincers sprang for my head and torso. Pain blossomed in my shoulders as pressure ground lower on my Kevlar sides. Its eyes sped greedily as it fed on my agony and terror.

My binding finally touched in a beautiful dark green circle, and for one triumphant moment I held the demon, though it held me. Its uppermost pincers were frozen in my curls. Then, Finn's rifle blasted deep inside the roiling cloud of the demon. Deadly arms, the nebulous mass, and rolling eyeballs winked into nothingness.

Panic and dread eased out of me, leaving only the

sharp pain of bleeding holes in my shoulders. The world seemed to lag for a moment, and I continued to hold the Dur-Alf realm, ready for another binding spell. My mind spun, trying to reconcile my safety against the emotions which had consumed me a moment before.

I'd had my first encounter with a demon and nearly died. If it weren't for Finn and his big gun, I would have. I shivered and focused on David, who was peering down at his chest.

Fitz whimpered at the far corner, hastily scratching a new sigil on the wall with a ball of charcoal.

"No you don't." I unleashed the binding I'd prepared for the demon. It wavered against his hoodie, then broke through some weakened ward and wrapped Fritz tight. He dropped into a rack of metal displays with a clatter.

"David?" Pyre's tone had no sense of urgency as she walked toward him.

"Through the tie. The red and blue one. Missed the jacket, so there's that." He smiled as if to be cavalier, but there was pain in his expression.

"You should sit for a moment." Pyre glanced over at the wall. So, she had seen it move as well.

"I should sit." David's legs folded carefully, but he sat abruptly on the dusty floor where he'd been standing.

Marie patted his shoulder and passed him to search out Fitz among the debris. "Tomas, get us local FBI over here, and squelch whatever local enforcement is sending. I'm sure someone heard the gunfire. This bay needs a tight inventory."

I headed for David. "Are you okay?" Blood had soaked his shirt and his tie. From the depth that demon's finger had plunged, anyone other than a vampire or werewolf would be dead or dying. I couldn't say about Marie, since the oldest rumors labeled dragon shifters as immortal.

He forced an exaggerated smile. "I am thirsty."

I rolled my eyes. "Sorry, that's not happening." My perception of vampires had changed from distrust or disgust to actually caring what happened to David. "You'll heal?" I really didn't know much about vampires, but he appeared to be in rough shape.

"Yes. Thanks." David closed his eyes and I took it as a cue to let him rest.

"I've never seen a sigil do that." Finn shouldered his rifle as he spoke and watched our suspect. I joined him.

Marie knelt by the immobilized Fitz, who laid wrapped in my full binding. Holding it would weary me after a while. Simple cuffs would likely suffice on a mundane. She pushed aside a wire grid wall with ease. His eyes were wide enough to show white, and his gaze stared at the ceiling. "Mr. Dunn. We're going to have some questions for you." She glanced at me and nodded. I released my binding.

"What—?" He scrambled back, his focus not on Marie, but behind where the demon had been. "Is it gone? What was that?"

"It is gone." Marie spoke with quiet reassurance. Sometimes during a chase or shootout, emotions rise so high that detectives or officers can become aggressive. She obviously did not have that flaw. "It came from the sigil you created. Do you understand that?" She rose as Fitz scrambled to his feet, trapped in the corner.

"No, it couldn't." He peered now at me and Finn. "That was just a ritual from a Zoroastrian magi. It just lets me move through . . ." His lips pursed and he studied Marie. He'd painted a silver sigil on the front of his hoodie. It looked scraped. Perhaps that had kept my binding from attaching the first time. "You are FBI."

"Yes. Your Akkadian sigil created other problems, at the museum and at the bank."

His expression sagged slightly and he glanced down to the left. "Something was there, at the . . ." Fitz inhaled quickly and tightened his expression. "I don't know what you're talking about." Then his eyes flicked to the far wall where we'd first seen him.

I moved toward the satchel which I'd seen him drop. Out of caution, I tugged at Dur-Alf to search for wards.

I picked up a folded piece of paper that had been dropped on the floor.

Marie echoed in the comms. "Mr. Dunn, what you've unleashed with your sigil matters far more to me than whatever you've stolen. Where did you learn it?"

A plastic bin against the wall held two rolled up paintings and a gold or bronze statue. I ignored those and grabbed the black bag which might have been a man's purse from the look of it.

Fitz remained silent, and Marie sighed over the comms. "I had hoped we could at least make sure that no one else will use the same sigil. That is truly my focus."

"They won't," he said with an arrogant tone.

The satchel had three Ziplocs in it, and I recognized the museum ring immediately. The reek of stale sweat eased out from under my Kevlar, but the air in the bay had soured with a fouler odor. Perhaps it came from David's blood, his healing, or the demon.

Marie spoke in that heavy voice she had used on Jack Darcy. "What does the sigil do?" I spun as her tone changed.

Fitz's face washed into a lax, flaccid expression. "It lets me move walls or reach through them." He spoke in a dull, compliant tone.

"Where did you learn about that sigil?"

"In a book I stole from Father Reyna."

"Where is this book?"

"Buried under the fireplace in our family home in Serbia."

"Address?" Her voice continued to compel the man, and his responses proved his inability to resist. I shivered at that kind of magic and had a moment of gratitude that Marie could get the answers, but that the Consociation limited the use.

I hesitated to approach her with the satchel and paper until she finished. Finn, too, remained where he was in the middle of the bay. David appeared to be meditating.

"Thank you, Mr. Dunn." Her normal tone had returned. "Tomas?"

"Sending the coordinates to Stacey now." The comms crackled.

"What happened?" His eyes had gone wide again, but now they were focused on Marie. Fitz's voice croaked. "How—"

"Mr. Dunn, or whoever you really are, you have become a rather dire security risk. You will have some options, but those aren't mine to offer. A transport will be here in a few minutes, and everything will be explained in time. I'm sorry." Marie's voice had a tone of remorse that grew stronger at the end. Whatever the Consociation did with 'dire security risk' prisoners, I couldn't imagine.

"I don't understand." He appeared frantic, ready to bolt.

I readied my fingers to pull another binding from Dur-Alf, but Finn stepped forward with zip ties.

Marie put her hand out, warning Fitz back. "You will. In time." She stopped him as he lurched and easily pinned him for Finn to cuff him. "Have a seat, Mr. Dunn." Pushing on his shoulders, she forced him down. His expression had lost any hint of the cool bravado he'd sported earlier; instead, he grimaced in fear at her touch.

I might have felt some pity for him if I couldn't still remember the haunting expression on the face of Brigid, the daughter of Heather Norris, not to mention the people affected by the murdered security guards at the bank, and their manager. They likely had loved ones and family who would never know the full story. At least we'd stopped it, and no one else would die during Fitz Dunn's thefts.

"Tomas, ETAs?" Marie motioned for me to put the satchel down, so I walked over and dropped it on the plastic bin.

"They'll pick up your suspect in four minutes. Local FBI will relieve you at the storage in fifty. I've turned around and am heading back to the office."

I unfolded the paper. A large sheet had sketched plans for a building. Some were notated with room names, times, and measurements. I quickly recognized the museum and the handwriting.

Marie frowned. "David and I will watch our friend. You two grab some pizza or something and bring it back. I'm starving."

Pizza? I nearly swooned.

David didn't open his eyes. "Pineapple and ham."

Finn grimaced, so I returned the same. He nodded toward the opening. "He's joking. One mushroom and one pepperoni. That okay?"

I nodded and waved the paper. "Marie?"

She turned. "What's that?"

"Plans for the museum, times, and measurements — in Jack's handwriting."

Marie glanced back at Fitz Dunn. "Good work."

I skipped over to join Finn and tucked the map in my jacket.

"No garlic sauce." David sounded better; he was joking

because garlic didn't actually work against vampires. That much I knew.

We walked around the corner, and I felt the day's use of magic wear on my energy. Food and water would help. The gray sky of dusk had triggered lighting above the buildings.

"What will happen to him? Fitz or whatever his name is."

Finn nodded. "The Consociation can't have knowledge of that sigil out there. If he chooses to lose his memories, the FBI will be allowed to take him into custody. I don't know the details."

"Have you ever heard of a sigil that could do that? Move him through walls? Move walls? Whatever it did?" I hadn't, and still didn't understand the mechanics. How could he pick up something in the safe-deposit box?

"New to me." Finn sighed. "Search sacred texts, Zoroastrianism based on the comment he made. The *Book of Arda Viraf* doesn't mention it, though I wonder about the context now."

Inside, I groaned at the amount of research I still had ahead of me before I ever got close to the level the rest of the team appeared to have. It felt dishonest being this ignorant of my job, and I hated that.

"I wonder if Jack timed his theft with Mr. Dunn's?" Finn stared ahead as he spoke.

I had considered the same. Jack had stolen the items and stashed them in the locker that same day. Perhaps he took them when the walking corpse had shown up. "That would be smart, to leave all the blame on someone else."

We reached the corner of the last building and could make out a motion over by the gate. Lights from the building illuminated a pimply-faced employee standing near the Jeep and eying the gate. David whistled to catch his attention, then flashed his badge. "Open the gate."

It took another wave of the badge before the young man started tapping in codes on the console. We arrived as the gate made a nasty grinding noise, clicked, and rolled backward.

Finn smiled as we approached. "Hey, we're going to have to cordon off this area. More FBI are coming. Can you hang out at the office in case they need keys or something? I don't know what time you usually leave."

"Yeah, sure." The employee glanced between Finn's dreads and the Kevlar vest. "What happened?"

"Sorry. Can't." Finn shrugged and patted the man on the shoulder. "Just chill for a bit, okay?"

The employee nodded, turning to head up to the office.

Finn opened the back door and slid his weapon over the seats, arranging it among the go bags. I assumed he was driving and circled around to the other side.

When I climbed into the passenger seat, I could smell David's mints. "Will David be okay?"

Finn started up the engine. "Yep. Vampires are tougher than a werewolf. He'll be ready for pizza when we get back."

I found that odd, but it was obvious I knew nothing about vampires. I would learn. "Why didn't Marie's bullets work? Did she miss?"

Finn snorted as he turned around. "Hardly. She's the best shot of all of us. Even our bullets on a demon are not a sure thing. Especially if they can phase their form. Gas to solid and back. Even solid, it often takes more than one to take one down."

He stopped at the road. "Find us a place?"

I winced and pulled out my iPhone to search pizza on Google. "Phase?" The only references to demons had been more on their ability to alter and feed on emotion rather than various physical shapes. I had assumed wrong from the sole illustration I had seen.

"The Tarus realm embodies change. Many of the old arcane were focused on those aspects. Demons represent that facet of the realm."

I gestured to the right, back along the direction we'd come.

Finn pulled onto the road. "A demon's purpose and demeanor are as likely to be in flux as well. They feed on emotion, but they might be secretive or outright hostile, such as the one we destroyed."

I could study demons in Tomas's archives later. It felt oddly normal to be heading off for pizza. After finishing my first bizarre case, I welcomed a simple food run. The Consociation and FBI would handle the rest. Finn didn't drive like a maniac, so I relaxed into my seat. I'd be sleeping in my own bed tonight.

I pointed at the oncoming red and green taco truck. "Is that . . .?" I could barely see a shadow over the steering wheel; perhaps a hood as we passed.

Finn laughed. "We can't leave David's blood around, nor our bullets."

CHAPTER
NINETEEN

"Kristen Winters."

Assistant Director Stacey Lockhart had an office on the floor above Pyre's Pups. David had given me the instructions to come up here, and the whole way I'd been sure he was pranking me. After a day off, you wouldn't know a demon had stuck a finger in his chest from the way he acted. I'd called Finn, but he was off today and his phone had gone to voice mail.

"Yes, Ma'am." I swallowed, unsure what I should call her.

Stacey was tall with an athletic build. She wore her sandy brown hair in a short trim at the neck that made me want to pull my curls back. Beside the unadorned window behind her, she had a bare bookshelf. The room held nothing more than that empty piece of furniture and the desk she sat at. No chairs for guests. It was a barren contrast to Marie's tightly cluttered office.

"Settling in? Pyre giving you any trouble?" She studied me and squinted her dark green eyes slightly at the last question.

Why would she ask that? "No. I'm getting along with everyone." I hoped.

"Good." Stacey's desk held only a framed picture and a tablet. Her elbows rested on the arms of her chair. "Pyre's reports of the mission regard you favorably. Your report was very — dry. Brief."

I forced my hands to stay at my sides and not fidget with my curls. "Are there points I should have elaborated on?"

Her eyes dilated, but her expression remained unreadable. My last experience with a werewolf had me on edge. My mind began to expand her face into jowls and lengthen her arms.

She attempted a light smile. "I just understand how this might be jarring."

Fighting a revenant, a draugr, and a demon? "Yes." Jarring didn't cover the terror that had surfaced in some of my dreams. I hadn't had nightmares since after the werewolf, and now they cropped up to wake me in the early morning hours. Despite Herta's healing, my upper arms hurt where the demon's claws had pierced me.

"Working with a dragon a problem?" Stacey's tone at the end of the sentence denoted a definite disdain.

"No, I'm fine with Marie — Agent Pyre. I never would have imagined I would be meeting one, let alone working . . . No, it's fine. Exciting." I was babbling.

Again Stacey's eyes flashed. "Very well. Yes, I'd like more detail in further reports." She scooped up her pad and turned it on. "That will be all."

"Yes, Ma'am." I held my breath until I closed her office door behind me. What did Stacey have against Pyre?

I'd spent a rather enjoyable quiet day meandering through Tomas's archives until now. Coming back from the bathroom to have David tell me Stacey wanted me in her office had been off-putting, but now I found myself distressed. I had just started to feel like one of the team. Stacey reminded me of the politics that always exist in any division or department.

Leaving Colorado had been a commitment, though I'd assumed with the FBI I could find an office closer to Jade in a couple years. That prospect had been destroyed the first day with Pyre's Pups. Our first case had me hooked. I couldn't let people face the kinds of horrors I'd seen. The mundanes and other witches deserved some semblance of peace, at least from that.

When I exited the elevator, our floor was empty, as usual. I'd never seen another soul go in or out a door at the other end of the corridor. My pace slowed as I passed Tomas's door and approached our office. I hated politics.

Marie and David sat on the edge of Finn's desk in the back of the room. They were silent as I stepped inside and closed the door. They had to know about Stacey's feelings for Marie.

"All good?" Marie asked.

I smiled, though I squirmed inside. "Yeah. She wants more detail in my reports." My fingers trailed along the edge of my desk. I took a deep breath and shook my head. "Marie, I don't know what's going on between you and Stacey, but she was digging for some kind of complaint."

David rolled his head back and groaned. Marie smiled. "David lost the bet; he's buying dinner and the rounds tonight. C'mon, grab your purse. Finn and Gary are waiting for us."

"Just stab me through the heart, again." David mocked a glare at me. "It took me three weeks before I told Pyre. I was sure you could hold out for three days."

I blushed and suppressed a happy chuckle at David losing the bet. Marie knew and didn't care about Stacey's issues. I was glad I had said something. We headed out of the office in a group, and I felt the warmth of going out with the team. In a short few days I felt like I'd settled into Pyre's Pups as one of their own. I still had a lot to learn about the cases they might be up against, but I'd proved myself able enough that I wasn't floundering.

Dinner turned out to be at a restaurant with outdoor seating beside the little airport we'd flown out of. The little jet hadn't been that bad. We'd be using it again; Pyre's Pups covered all the Americas.

Finn and Gary had saved a table by the railing. Finn's husband was shorter than him with a bit more paunch and more gray than brown in his beard. He was laughing and holding Finn's hand as we walked out onto the patio.

"David lost the bet," Marie announced as we walked up.

Gary appeared confused and Finn patted his hand. "Office politics. Let me introduce you to our new darling, Kristen."

They both stood, and Gary put both hands on mine. "Pleasure's mine. Finn says you're fitting in right off the bat." He grinned. "Not like that one." He winked at David. "Did you have to move to Atlanta, or are you local?"

I warmed to Gary immediately, and sat next to him after he patted the seat beside him. He sipped wine as we talked.

A server came to our table, and David monopolized the young man with an interrogation on available fine wines.

Marie smiled at the server. "Loblolly, double IPA." She turned to me. "It's a great local beer."

When the server glanced at me to order, I tilted my head toward my boss. "Great minds drink alike."

Finn and Gary groaned in unison as the server frowned, not understanding.

I flushed, clarifying, "I'll have the same."

Demon

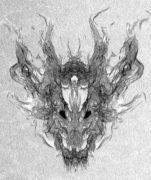

A demon is a rare inhabitant of the Tarus Realm who can be summoned to the Earth realm or cross of its own intent if given an opening. [1]

Their summoned forms often are a nightmarish mirror of their summoner with features designed to terrorize, such as claws, fangs, and horns. [1][2] Highly intelligent, they feed on strong emotions such as panic or rage. [2][3]

They are reported to rely on physical attributes for attack, but have been known to compel humans to act out their violence. [2][3]

(Cont. next page; Accounts of Demons in Tarus)

[1] Read Tinkanchtners's The Art of Demonic Summoning

[2] Read Kizurra's Referene on Tarus Cryptids Page 26 to 47

[2] Read Carey's Of Demons and Jinns

Dragon-shifter

The portion of a dragon exposed in the Earth realm which can mimic the aspect of a human.

Most of what is known about dragon-shifters has come from archaic grimoires with questionable translations. [1][2] There is at least one resident on Earth to coordinate with the Consociation. [3] Reportedly, a dragon-shifter is an exact replica of a human, unless they intend otherwise. [2][4] A witch would know on contact.

The details of their craft ability are shrouded in myth due to their self-expulsion from the Earth realm prior to the Akkadian wars was preceded by a slow withdrawal during the prior era. [1][2][4] They openly apologize for their interference with man, resulting in the rituals that brought about the vampires and werewolves. [3][5]

(Cont. next page; Role in Consociation)

[1] Read Yin's Volume IV of Realm Studies Pages 1340 to 1489
[2] Read Wooley's Anecdotal Studies of Salmhalla
[3] Read Ferno's Presentation of the Consociation
[4] Read Inhai Du Anya's Scriptures of the High Dragons Page 1-72
[5] Read Sover's On Madness

Draugr / Draughr

A common inhabitant of Tarus who can be summoned to the Earth realm, or cross of its own intent if given an opening.

Territorial they tend toward an unusual compunction to protect valuables.

Tall and strong they present as humanoid on Earth with no skin and sharp black nails. They possess reflexes and speed beyond humans.[1] Savage and instinctual on a physical level. Relatively low intelligence.

Magical or Arcane abilities: None

Note the Akkadian ritual listed in the 1911 appendix

[1] Read Macrin's Journal for an in-depth biological reference compilation of Merfolk research of the Draugr

Dwarf / Dwarves

Humanoid residents of Dur-Alf with a proclivity for exploration and research. Their earliest interactions with humans caused a wider disturbance than expected and their own sanctions for crossing to Earth were ignored by many of their more independant scholars and explorers. Brief conflicts existed between individuals as witches developed the ability to pass into the Dur-Alf realm.

Small in mass and stature, their biology is similar to Earth mammals. [1]

Conflicts erupted between humans and dwarves [2] as human witches and arcane users began to cross realms. Dwarves are especially biased against vampires.

(Cont. next page; Magical and Arcane usage)

[1] Read Macrin's *Understanding Dwarven Physiology and Psyche*

[2] Read Thant's *War on Human Mutation*

Kuru Kuru

Mammallian bipedal residents of Dur-Alf though the only known description of their physical resemblance comes from two sources and both differ slightly. [1][2]

The Dwarves do acknowledge their presence and the Kuru Kuru have been given access to the Consociation. [3] They speak only to the Dragon delegation there and have some relationship with Dragons. [4]

Small in mass and stature, their biology is similar to Earth mammals with a flattened muzzle. Reports differ on fur (pictured), or with feathers. [1][2][3]

(Cont. next page; Magical suppositions)

[1] Read Kainin's Guide to Dur-Alf, Eden of the Realms

[2] Read Emily Randolp's Memoirs Among the Sprites

[3] Read Daesalu's Biography of Talat

[4] Read Ono Seyo's Conspiracy of the Consociation

Merfolk / Mer

Mer, called Merfolk by the Consociation, have the ability to transform into similar mammalian shapes upon interrealm movement. [1]

Little is known about their unaltered form except that it is a sea mammal of some type, hypothesized to be porpoise-like. [2]

Their longstanding habitation of Earth's oceans ceased at the point when Earth witches and arcane users began using the Mer realm in magic which coincided with the interrealm movement of humans to Dur-Alf. [3] Merfolk returned to Earth during the formation of the Consociation at the urging of the dwarves with whom they had long enjoyed diplomacy and trade. [4]

Many Mer research and work on Earth as part of their proposal to the Consociation for admittance. [5]

(Cont. next page; the impact of Merfolk on magical use by witches and the arcane)

[1] Read Sienna's Treatise on Earth's Devastation

[2] Read Tino Vangian Biography of Venis: Traitor of Mer

[3] Read Sienna's Treatise on Mer Isolation

[4] Read Tino Vangian Biography of Venis: Traitor of Mer

[5] Read Tino Vangian's Biograpy of Sienna

Revenant

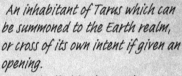

An inhabitant of Tarus which can be summoned to the Earth realm, or cross of its own intent if given an opening.

Disembodied in the Earth realm, they will seek to possess a humanoid corpse, or living entities with a weakened consciousness such as comotose or those near death.

Their corporeal control depends greatly on their prior experience.[1]

They range in intelligence and will avoid confrontation where possible.

Expellation is relatively simple depending on the skill of the witch.[2] Vampires have an innate ability to remove Revenants from their possessed hosts.

Magical or Arcane abilities: None

[1] Read Rasputin's Walks Among the Undead for a detailed observance of summoned Revenants

[2] See Appendix from 1892 - reference Possession

Vampire

   A vampire is a human-born crossover to the Tarus realm. They are infected with a Tarus symbiotic life form initially misunderstood as a form of magic inherited from Tarus. [1] The infection can be summoned, gained through prolonged contact with Tarus, or transferred by blood-to-blood transfer with a vampire. [2]

   The human cells are mutated to a far more resilient state and can be controlled to an extent which allows the vampire to change facial features and extend their life. [1] [3] Strength and speed are are increased with minimal muscular and bone alterations. [4] Vampires are entirely resistant to infection, disease, and toxins. [3] Mental acuity does not change. Emotional reactions remain, though extended life spans have brought interesting results. [1] [3] [4] [5]

      (Cont. next page; the Tarus symbiote)

[1] Read Tonsun's Illuminating the Mystery

[2] Read William Beckett's Becoming a Legend

[3] Read Annan's Study on Mutation

[4] Read Anonymous Confessions of Self-Hatred

[5] Read Maorin's Sapien Emotive Reponses Pages 21-88

Werewolf / Dreamer / Hunter

Born human they have developed a psychic and realm connection to Ya Keya. They are affected by their interactions and develop biological alterations. The connection can be summoned, by a ritual interaction with the bodily fluids of a mature werewolf, or through intense submersion in Ya Keya.[1] Longevity varies [2]

Transmuted form:
They gain 15-20% more mass directly from the Ya Keya realm. Reflexes, strength, and speed increase by 10-30% beyond their human norms. Eyesight and hearing are more acute though more age dependant than other attributes.[2]

(Cont. next page; loss of Magic and Arcane usage)

[1] Read Kizurra's History of Akkadian Werewolves - the Dawn

[2] Read Demot's Monograph for an in-depth biological reference

Dur-Alf

Visible indications are a dark-green color and a crumbling or dusty consistency.

Dur-Alf is a planet realm similar to Earth in that it orbits a singular star; it is the fourth of eight known bodies in the system and does not have any satellites. There are major land-locked bodies of water and large polar ice caps. [1] Rivers and lakes abound in most regions except near equatorial deserts. The seasons are mild, and wildlife is plentiful. [1] [2] The only known transplants from Earth are kestrels and a variety of water birds including swans, geese, ducks, and kingfishers. [1] [2] [3]

Humans are no longer welcome or tolerated in the Dur-Alf realm. [4]

Known bordering realms: Earth, Mer, Salmhalla, Mer, and Tique (described as a hostile realm [5]).

(Cont. next page; Known Species)

[1] Read Kainan's Guide to Dur-Alf; Eden of the Realms

[2] Read Emily Randalp's Memoirs Among the Sprites

[3] Read Yin's Volume VI of Realm Studies Pages 1289 to 1402

[4] Read Consociation Guidelines for Interrealm Treaties. Page 157.

[5] Read Yin's Volume VIII of Realm Studies Page 44 to 399

Haven

Visible indication is a white mist of a thick consistency reminding some observers of cotton candy.

Haven is a plane realm of breathable air, moisture in the form of clouds or mist, and no gravity. The ambient light is bright. No lifeforms or other identifying components have been found in the realm. [1][2][3]

Dwarves and Merfolk have often used Earth merely to experience the realm. [3][4] Other than the magic available by touching the realm, little of use exists there.

Hypothesises exist as to alternates states. [3][5][6]

Known bordering realms: Earth, Salmhalla, and Tarus.

(Cont. next page; Consociation Prohibitions)

[1] Read Yin's Volume III of Realm Studies. Pages 239 to 449 and appendix A

[2] Read Maorin's A Bridge to Haven; the Trail of Tears and Tribulations

[3] Read Innatala's Forgotten Path

[4] Read Soen's Research on Haven

[5] Read Ilionor's Mystics Realm

[6] Read Iai's Casual Observances and Lost Myths

Mer / Ishi-Iyai-Eyai-I

Visible indication is a blue-green liquid of a denser consistency than water.

Mer is a planet realm, a water-encased world with islands and some non-aquatic life. [1] Mer is the third planet from a hot star with higher than Earth surface temperatures and a single satellite. [2] Like Earth's humans, merfolk are the single indigenous intelligent life. Non-indigenous sentient life include the porpoises and whales, two of the numerous transplanted species between the two realms. [2]

No reported excursions into the realm have survived, and the merfolk refuse access to the realm, part of their reasoning for joining the Consociation.

Known bordering realms: Dur-Alf, Earth, and Tarus.

Interrealm travel from Earth by humans is prohibited by the Consociation Regulations. [4]

(Cont. next page; historical connection to Earth and Dur-Alf)

[1] Read Sienna's Treatise on Mer Isolation

[2] Read Tino Vangian Biography of Venis: Traitor of Mer

[4] Read Consociation Guidelines for Interrealm Treaties. Page 114.

Salmhalla

Indications include a liquid gold which is burning hot to the touch. [1]

Salmhalla is a plane of ambient sunlight and hot air temperatures. [1] [2] The plane contains a wide range of Earth-like terrains but predominantly includes mountains and grassy hills. [1] [2] [3] Several large water bodies have been detailed, but none rise to the level of oceans. [2] [3] [4] [5]

Consociation guidelines prohibit interaction with the realm and dragons enforce this edict. [6]

Known infringements have resulted in death, disappearance, mental illness, and loss of memory.

(Cont. next page; Known, theorized, and postulated magics connected to the Salmhalla realm)

[1] Read Yin's Volume IV of Realm Studies. Pages 1121 to 1349 and appendix C

[2] Read Inhai Du Anya's Scriptures of the High Dragons. Pages 89 to 97.

[3] Read Serjin's Testimonials

[4] Read Ilionor's Biography of Reshin. Pages 245 to 271.

[5] Read Wooley's Anecdotal Studies of Salmhalla

[6] Read Consociation Guidelines for Interrealm Treaties. Page 57.

Tarus

Visible indications are a dark-gray color and a misty consistency with glittering elements akin pin head.

Tarus is a plane realm with no ambient lighting and an oxygen-rich atmosphere. [1][2] Theories vary that the indigenous lifeforms have abilities to perceive lower frequency magnetic waves, have other senses, or solely rely on tactile and auditory senses. [2][3][4] Most grimoires record little of verifiable evidence, but specimens from the realm have been studied extensively by multiple races. [5][6] A rocky, waterless terrain is a commonly accepted description. [2][4]

Known bordering realms: Earth, Haven, and Ya Keya.

(Cont. next page; Consociation Prohibitions)

[1] Read Yin's Volume II of Realm Studies. Pages 71 to 549 and appendix B

[2] Read Rasputin's Walks Among the Undead, the annotated version.

[3] Read Serjin's Agreements in Darkness

[4] Read Ilionor's Dedication

[5] Read Finyai's Tarus Biology

[6] Read Ted Dansworth's Research of Tarus Corporeal

Ya Keya

Indications include a light gray mist which is moist to the touch.

Considered the hunter's dream world, it is a plane of blue gray twilight according to numerous excursions including a Merfolk expedition led by Antre.[1] The plane contains a wide range of Earth-like terrains but predominantly includes forests, plains, and savannahs. No large water bodies have ever been detailed, but marshes and bogs were noted. [2]

Continued interaction with the plane consistently results in a transmutation on a cellular level and the werewolf's bodily fluids become contagious.[3] Longevity and increased metabolic functions have been studied extensively. [4] [5]

Witches and Merfolk have lost all abilities to interact with the realms once transmutation has occurred.

(Cont. next page; Known Inhabitants of Ya Keya)

[1] Read Antre's paper on To Ya Keya: Sacrifice and Betrayal

[2] Read Yin's Volume III of Realm Studies

[3] Read Jayne Dunham's Voyage Home

[4] Read Kizurra's History of Akkadian Werewolves - the Dawn

[5] Read Demot's Monograph for an in-depth biological reference

ALSO BY KEVIN A DAVIS

Please head to my website and join my mailing list if you'd like to be kept up to date on this series or my other books.

Khimmer Chronicles

Wight's Wrath - Book One

Death's Contract - Book Two

Fate's Betrayal - Book Three

High Fae's Quest - Book Four

Friday's Fifth - Book Five

Nyx's Blade - The Origin Story

AngelSong Series

Penumbra - Book One

Red Tempest - Book Two

Coerced - Book Three

Demons' Lair - Book Four

Infrared - Book Five

If you haven't read the Origin story of the **AngelSong** series, *Shattered Blood*, then download a free ebook or purchase the paperback or audible on Amazon.

Website KevinArthurDavis.com
Facebook @KevinArthurDavis
KevinADavis on Instagram
KevinADavisUF on Twitter

ACKNOWLEDGMENTS

April appears to enjoy the DRC files and has had a strong hand in helping develop some aspects. Her proofing alone has helped avoid some embarrassing mistakes.

Robyn Huss, my editor, weaves her own magic on my stories. If you enjoy this, it's largely due to her. If you're a writer, I encourage you to look at some of the opportunities she offers - http://www.hussediting.com/

The Fireside Group; Siena, Rosemary, Mark, Tim, Vail, and Katharine keep me challenged to do better. Arrash and Michele from Jody Lynn Nye's DragonCon workshop keep me on task with the most intricate details and loving support. Dianne and Brett from Apex have been there for me.

I still miss David Farland's gentle mentorship. Please pick up one of his books and enjoy the magic he endowed upon the world. Writers, study his lessons at Apex Writers.

Jody Lynn Nye's workshop will always be my go to suggestion for an in-person critique for any aspiring writers. Her insight is invaluable.

The wonderful cover art is by Rebekah at VividCovers! Consider her for your next design.

Thank you.

www.ingramcontent.com/pod-product-compliance
Lightning Source LLC
Jackson TN
JSHW081127170225
78991JS00002B/23